ALSO BY

JASMINE WARGA

My Heart and Other Black Holes

HERE
WE
ARE
nOw

Jasmine Warga

BALZER + BRAY
An Imprint of HarperCollins*Publishers*

Balzer + Bray is an imprint of HarperCollins Publishers.

Here We Are Now
Text copyright © 2017 by Jasmine Warga
Illustrations copyright © 2017 by Monica Ramos
www.epicreads.com

ISBN 978-0-06-232470-2 (hardcover)
ISBN 978-0-06-269404-1 (international edition)

Typography by Torborg Davern
17 18 19 20 21   PC/LSCH   10 9 8 7 6 5 4 3 2 1

First Edition

*To Greg, for giving me that EP ten years ago
and for everything after*

DAY ONE

(In Which a Stranger Who Was Not Really a Stranger Knocked on My Door)

I.

There are people that you never expect to show up on your doorstep. For me, this list begins with the pope, the president, and my second-grade teacher, Mrs. Jenkins, because she absolutely hated me.

He would've been somewhere on my Most Unlikely List. Probably top ten. But there was a time, not so long ago, when he wouldn't have been on that list. There was actually a time when I would camp out by the window, willing him to pull up into the driveway. I always imagined him driving a black Mustang with a loud, rumbling engine. I used to picture him in the driver's seat, his sunglasses pushed up in his messy pale corn-colored hair, wearing his mint green plaid pajama pants that had become so iconic thanks to the *Rolling Stone* photo shoot.

But after three years of unanswered letter after unanswered letter, I'd finally accepted that it was never going to happen.

Until it did.

When I heard the first knock, I freaked out. We weren't expecting any guests and I have the type of brain that always goes to the Absolute Worst-Case Scenario. And so I did what anyone would do when they believe someone is attempting to break into their house and hack them to death with a chainsaw—I called for help.

"Harlow?" I called out. She was in the kitchen whipping up a batch of her pistachio cupcakes with buttercream icing.

"Yes?" she answered over the noisy whirl of the electric mixer and the Dresden Dolls record that was turned on full blast. Amanda Palmer was crooning about jeeps and betrayal. Harlow was in a phase where she was both nursing a major crush on Amanda Palmer and wanting to be Amanda Palmer.

"I think there's someone at the door."

I heard the electric mixer switch off. "Yeah. I thought I heard a knock. Are you expecting anyone?"

I reclined farther into the couch and pressed pause on

Netflix, frantically trying to remember the name of an artsy French movie that I could turn on. If Harlow and I were about to be savagely murdered by a serial killer, I wanted to be remembered for my unimpeachable taste in foreign cinema, not my penchant for reality cooking competitions. "No," I answered, this time lowering my voice in case said murderer was eavesdropping on us. "Are you?"

Harlow walked into the living room. My mother's paisley-patterned cooking apron was draped over Harlow's tiny frame, sporting some fresh flour splotches. There was also a sliver of icing on the left side of her face. Harlow was a terrific baker, albeit not a neat one. "Nope. I told Quinn she could come over later for cupcakes and pizza, but she doesn't get off work until six." Harlow pulled her phone out of the back pocket of her frayed denim shorts, which she was wearing over polka-dotted tights. "What time is it, anyway?"

I glanced at the cable box. "Twelve thirty-one. Definitely not six."

"Okay. So it isn't Quinn. But that doesn't mean it's Charles Manson."

Quinn was Harlow's girlfriend. And while she wasn't Charles Manson, she did sort of terrify me. They'd been together seven and a half months, and I still didn't feel confident that Quinn liked me. I worried that Quinn didn't find me edgy or interesting enough, or worse, thought I was a complete nutball. How I responded to situations like the one that was presently unfolding did not bode well for my score on the nutball scale.

"Tal," Harlow said, using her knowing, level voice with me. "Why don't you just go open the door and see who it is? I'll be right here."

I bit my bottom lip and stared at the frozen image of Gordon Ramsay on the television screen. I hadn't yet switched over to the French new wave film whose title I couldn't remember.

The doorbell rang again.

"Tal," Harlow repeated. "Answer the door."

"But we don't know who it is."

We'd entered our usual call-and-response pattern. I like to think that's one of the hallmarks of Bestfrienddom—that comfortable circular conversation.

She sighed and I watched her flip her phone over in her hands. I had a sinking feeling that she was debating whether or not to text Quinn and tell her I was being a complete nutball. Great.

The only thing worse than my best friend being infinitely cooler than me was that now she had a girlfriend who was infinitely cooler than both of us. And I could feel Harlow slipping away—slowly, but still slipping. Being pulled into the orbit of Quinn and Quinn's alluring pack of friends. It terrified me.

In the past few months, something had shifted between Harlow and me. It was difficult to put a finger on. It wasn't like an earthquake or anything that dramatic, but there was a fissure. Before, I had been the first person Harlow told everything to. And of course, I told her everything first too. Really, there wasn't anyone other than my mom who I confided in besides Harlow. Now that Harlow had Quinn, I was Harlow's second person. But she was still my first. And that made me feel sad.

No one wants to be in second place.

When Harlow had first come over today, she pretended like everything was normal. But I knew it was a tactic. Harlow didn't ever want to talk about what had changed between us. She wanted to keep on pretending like things were as they always had been, even though they clearly weren't.

I wondered if Harlow was only here now because Mom had called Harlow and asked her to come. I could easily imagine the phone call: "Harlow, dear," my mother would've said in her formal tone that she believed disguised her ever-present accent. "I'm going to be away for a few days in Paris, giving a lecture at the launch of a new gallery. Would you do me a huge favor and check in on Tal from time to time for me?"

"Yes. Of course, Dr. Abdallat," Harlow would've said, because despite the frayed denim jean shorts and polka-dotted tights and chipped dark nail polish, Harlow at her core was still the authority-pleasing third grader who turned in every book report a week before it was due. She was also one of the few people I knew who referred to my mother as Dr. Abdallat. Yes, she had a degree in art history and theory, but she was a professor, not a medical doctor.

"Okay. Fine. Let's just take a deep breath and behave like normal people," Harlow insisted. She marched toward the window. She pulled back the thin lavender curtain and let out a gasp.

"What is it?" I whispered, my body stiffening.

"Taliah Sahar Abdallat, you're going to want to see this."

My throat went dry. "Seriously, what is it?"

"Taliah." Her voice was rigid. "Come here."

I pulled myself up from the couch. I walked to stand beside her and looked out the window. The mid-summer daylight was bouncing off the window in a blinding fashion and I had to blink a few times to make sure my eyes were really seeing what I thought they were seeing.

It was him.

Three years too late.

Or really sixteen years too late if we're being honest.

But it was him.

Dear Julian Oliver,

I really don't know how to begin this letter other than to say, I think you're my dad. There is so much I want to say, but I felt the need to start with a neat and pretty and direct beginning. Something to get you hooked so you'll keep reading this letter until the end.

I like to imagine this is how you feel when you go about ordering the tracks for one of your albums. You select something nice and catchy for the beginning track and then slyly sandwich in some of the more meaningful but less flashy songs.

Now, before you throw this letter away, please hear me out. I'm sure you get deranged fan letters all the time, but that's not what this is. To be honest, I'm not even a huge fan of yours. I don't mean that in a bad way. I like your music just fine, but it's not like my favorite or anything. To be fair, that probably has a lot to do with the fact that my mother doesn't really let me listen to your genre of music much, which, after my recent discovery, is starting to make a lot more sense.

I guess I should mention that my mother is Dr. Lena Noura Abdallat. Ha! I bet I have your interest now, right?

Anyway, when I was snooping in her study I found a well-cataloged shoebox. (The shoebox was full of news clippings about you and your band. Cutouts of write-ups from Rolling Stone and the profile that the New York Times did on you a few years back. And then, buried under all the news clippings, there was a single letter from you to her. It was written on yellowed paper. Three lines only:

> *Lena,*
> *Please give me one more chance. This time it will be*
> *different. I promise.*
> *Always,*
> *Julian*

So you have to understand how my brain basically exploded at that moment. I stared at your photograph from one of the articles that had run in Rolling Stone and was amazed to see that we have the exact same eyes. I mean, exact same eyes, dude. And as you know, Mom is from Jordan, so that was always something I wondered about because Mom told me that my dad was someone she knew from back home. She claimed I was conceived (GROSS) when she went home for her mother's funeral, but like how many Jordanians do you know with icy blue eyes?

And then I did more research into you—thanks, Google— and found out that you are from none other than Oak Falls, Indiana. Guess what? Mom went to undergrad at Hampton University in, yup, Oak Falls, Indiana. I'm guessing that's where you guys met, right?

Basically, I want you to explain yourself. Or at least

answer my letter to tell me if I'm on the right track or not. You owe me some answers.

I know you are a busy man, so I've laid out my three most pressing questions below and would appreciate if you could contact me as soon as possible with the answers:

1) Are you my father?

2) Did you already know that you were my father?

3) What does my mom need to forgive you for?

Your maybe-possibly-probably daughter,
Taliah Sahar Abdallat

PS: I've included a recent photograph of Mom. She's a babe, right? Also, check it out—that's from an article she had published in Art History. You aren't the only rock star in this "family."

II.

clutched Harlow's shoulder. "Is that who I think it is?"

She reached out and squeezed my other hand. "That's a loaded question."

I thought of the famous photograph spread shot by Annie Leibovitz where Julian Oliver was holding a gun in his right hand and the neck of his guitar in his left. "Harlow."

"Taliah."

"Well, I think it is him. Pretty sure he's Julian Oliver. But I'm still unwilling to fully agree that he is who you think he is." She squeezed my hand again. "In that regard."

"In that regard," I repeated absently, and snuck another

glance at the willowy figure standing on my doorstep. I'd imagined this moment so many times, and now that it was finally here, I found it very difficult to be present in it. It almost felt as if I were watching a videotape of my life.

My mind repeated the same refrain over and over again: *Julian Oliver is standing on your doorstep.*

Julian Oliver of rock star fame.

Julian Oliver, my long-lost father.

You see, three years ago when I'd discovered The Shoebox in my mother's home studio/office—I obviously immediately shared this life-altering revelation with Harlow because she was and is my first-choice person. But analytical-to-a-fault Harlow hadn't been as convinced as me. Her arguments, presented below in no particular order, were valid:

1. Lots of people have glacier-like blue eyes and dimples in their right cheeks.
2. Mom could have been a huge hardcore fan of Staring Into the Abyss. A secret fan, but a die-hard one nonetheless. Lots of people were.
3. It was just very unfathomable and unlikely.
4. See point 3 and repeat it over and over and over again.

My counterpoints were as follows:

1. Yes, but there was still a startling resemblance. We even smiled in the same way. Didn't she see that? (She eventually admitted that she did, indeed, see it.

Especially the way both of our bottom lips curved slightly to the left, which served to further highlight the dimple in our right cheek.)

2. Mom hated rock music. This had been a point of contention between Mom and me for basically my whole life. I'd had to beg—I mean capital-*B* Beg—her to let me take piano lessons. And to this day, she only wanted me to listen to classical music and musical soundtracks. Any modern music I listened to was a secret affair. Her disdain for rock music had always seemed odd, and I remember one time when she had a very strong reaction to a Staring Into the Abyss song that came over the speakers when we were in a store. All this is to say, Mom's reactions to rock music, particularly Staring Into the Abyss, seemed suspiciously out of proportion.

3. Mom had completed her undergraduate studies at Hampton University, a private college nestled in the sleepy town of Oak Falls, Indiana. Guess where Julian Oliver was born and raised? Yup. You guessed it.

4. Sure, it was very unfathomable and unlikely, but so were many things that existed in this world, such as air travel, the smallpox vaccine, and the absolute perfection of Beyoncé.

Harlow dropped my hand. "You're going to answer the door, right?"

I nodded dumbly. "But what do I say?"

"Why don't you wait and see what he says?"

I stood frozen and she let out a loud sigh. "Taliah. You have to open the door. This is getting weird."

"Isn't it already crazy weird?"

"Yes," she said emphatically. "So there's no need to make it any more weird." And with that, Harlow pulled open the door.

Staring Into the Abyss

Staring Into the Abyss (S.I.T.A.) is an American indie rock band that was formed in Oak Falls, Indiana, in 1999. The band's lyrics, which have been described as "poetic, esoteric, and melancholy," are written and sung by Julian Oliver, the band's lead singer. Oliver also reportedly composes the vast majority of the band's music, though according to an interview with *Pitchfork* in 2011, Oliver is occasionally lent a hand, which most people took to be a nod to band member Marty St. Clair. The band has recorded four studio albums, the most popular of which is *Blind Windows*, which was released in July 2002, and includes the hit single "That Night." The band hasn't put out a new album since 2011 and there is much speculation about when or if a new record will be released.

BAND MEMBERS

Julian Oliver—lead vocals, guitar

Marty St. Clair—keyboard, bass, backup vocals

Chris Stevens—bass, backup vocals

Brett Bannister—drums, percussion

MUSICAL STYLE

The band has been compared to several other indie and alternative rock bands and musical acts, such as the National, the White Stripes, Neutral Milk Hotel, the Cure, and Wolf Parade. Oliver has cited Leonard Cohen and

Elliott Smith as major influences on his lyrical writing, as well as Isaac Brock. He has also mentioned drawing inspiration from William Blake, Anne Sexton, and William Faulkner. Given that the band's name is a direct reference to Friedrich Nietzsche, it is likely Oliver is also inspired by Nietzsche and other nineteenth-century philosophers. Because of Oliver's poetic, wistful, and obscure lyrics, he has developed an almost cult-like following of worship among his fans.

Due to some of the band's more hard-edged songs, they have also drawn comparisons to the Clash; one music review outlet once even went as far as to call Staring Into the Abyss a "doe-eyed version of a British punk grunge band. Sure, they have prettier, more esoteric lyrics, but at the end of the day, fans turn out for the same reason—to jump around to the jagged bass lines and thundering percussion."

DISCOGRAPHY

Winter in Indiana (2000)

Blind Windows (2002)

Fireproof (2007)

You'll Never See Me Again (2011)

III.

He looked slightly different from the numerous photos I'd seen of him online. But it was definitely him. Same shaggy pale blond hair that somehow managed to be long and short at the same time. (In the sunlight, I noticed a few gray streaks that never showed up in press photos.) Same globe-shaped, icy blue eyes—my eyes. Same freckled nose that hooked a little to the right. Same willowy frame with slightly hunched posture.

"Taliah?" he said. Looking back, I think he should've come up with a better line. After all, he was the one showing up on *my* doorstep.

I didn't say anything because I was, well, wholly unprepared.

"I'm Harlow," Harlow said, and opened the door wider. "And this is Taliah."

Julian kept his eyes trained on my face. "Wow. Holy shit. You look so much like your mother." He ran his hands through his hair. "Shit. Wait. I probably shouldn't curse in front of you, should I?" He smiled tentatively.

"I'm sixteen, not four," I managed to say. My voice was sharper than I'd intended it to be.

"Right." He nodded, clearly startled by my tone. "Is your mother home?"

The answer to his question was an easy no. Mom was across the Atlantic Ocean. She was speaking at the opening of some fancy new gallery in Paris, giving a talk on contemporary woven arts. So I should've been able to plainly tell him no, but I didn't. Because normally, you see, if a stranger asked me if my mother was home, I would've quickly said yes, even if she wasn't. I would've told the stranger that not only was my mother home, but so were ten other people, all armed with machetes and machine guns, thank you very much.

And the man standing before me was a stranger.

But he also wasn't.

This was all very freaking confusing.

The silence stretched between us, and finally Harlow

answered, "No. She's actually not home right now."

Julian rubbed the bottom of his chin and grimaced a little.

"You're both relieved and disappointed?" I said without thinking.

"Yes." He gave me the same tentative smile from earlier. "Exactly."

I shook my head and squinted past him into the sunlight. "Why are you here now?"

He shoved his hands into the pockets of his skinny black jeans. The pants were probably an inappropriate choice for most men of his age, but I guessed that the rules of fashion applied differently to rock stars, even aging ones. "Because, well . . . I don't really know how to say this."

"Just say it," I said.

"Your grandfather is dying."

"Um. That already happened. He died before I was born." *Jedde* had passed before my mother even immigrated to the United States. I only knew about him from photographs and stories my mother told. He had her same soft brown eyes. He had liked mint tea and the way the light looked in the late afternoon—the golden hour.

Julian swayed from side to side, switching the weight of his body from his left to right foot and back again. He frequently rocked like that when he was onstage. It was very freaking weird to watch him do that on my doorstep. "Not that grandfather. My father."

"Your father."

"Yes."

I widened my eyes. "Oh."

"Oh," Harlow echoed, the moment dawning on her too.

"So when you say my grandfather . . ."

"Yes," Julian Oliver said with a nod. "I believe your theory is right."

"My theory."

"Jeez," he said with a bit of a laugh. "You don't make things easy for a guy."

I watched him fidget on my doorstep. I didn't think he deserved easy after sixteen years of silence. He deserved hard. Trench warfare hard. Siberian winter hard. Capital-*H* effing Hard. "Why would I?"

He bit his lip. I recognized the nervous gesture. It was one of mine. "Touché."

After a few more beats of silence, he said, "But damn, kid, it is hot as hell out here. Can I at least come in and try to explain myself?"

"I guess," I said, despite the warning bells ringing in my head. I motioned toward the living room. "Come on in."

IV.

It was hard to reconcile all the conflicting emotions that were brewing inside of me. On one hand, I was pretty shocked and giddy that he had finally shown up. And even more giddy that all the suspicions I'd been harboring since I was thirteen years old seemed to be true and not just flights of adolescent fantasy.

I mean, I really was the daughter of a rock star. I allowed myself to have a Holy Hell moment before the anger set in. I was the daughter of a man who people camped out for hours outside of a venue to catch a glimpse of. People spent hours analyzing the lyrics to his iconic songs and then had those lyrics tattooed across their rib cages. People full-on worshipped him.

But the giddy surrealness of it all faded quickly to anger. Because if all my suspicions were correct, where had he been my whole life? Why had he abandoned my mother? Had he known she was pregnant? And why hadn't he answered any of my letters? Not. A. Single. Response.

He sat on the floral upholstered couch Mom and I had picked out from the Anthropologie catalog two years ago. His knees bounced up and down like he was having difficulty controlling his energy. I remembered how one *Rolling Stone* interviewer had described him as "manic."

"I can't believe you're here," I said. I was still standing, which I knew probably made this insanely weird moment even weirder. But I couldn't bring myself to sit.

Harlow, though, had plopped down in the wing-backed white leather chair that sat squarely across from the couch, folded her hands in her lap, and seemed to be perfectly content waiting for this conversation to unspool. She also took a not-so-discreet photograph of him with her phone and was presumably texting it to Quinn. I wanted to be mad, but I couldn't really blame her.

"I know," he said, not looking me in the eye. His focus darted around the room. He paused on a photograph of Mom and me taken on a trip to Hawaii last summer. "It must seem odd to you."

"Uh, yeah. That's an understatement. All of this seems beyond odd to me."

He turned to stare at the framed Quran passage that hung on the left wall. The dark ink of the Arabic calligraphy contrasted with the creamy parchment paper. Mom wasn't particularly religious. Actually, considering that she frequently had a glass of red wine with dinner, did not wear a hijab, and hardly ever attended a function at the mosque, it might be more precise to say Mom wasn't religious at all, but she was a tricky woman to figure out. Because while she was not overtly religious, and she never fasted during Ramadan, she still hosted late-evening dinners for single Muslim women. When I was little, I used to slip out of bed and scoot down the stairs, spying on them as they broke their fast with dates and water, later moving on to the lamb-stuffed okra and mounds of rice my mother had uncharacteristically cooked.

I'd once brought up all these contradictions to Harlow and she'd squinted at me and said, "Tal. Faith is a complicated thing." Which is a very Harlow thing to say.

I didn't exactly know what the Quran passage said, since I couldn't read Arabic. But ever since Harlow had said that, I'd translated the calligraphy to read: *Faith is a complicated thing.*

I glanced at Julian and thought: *Paternity is an uncomplicated thing. Fatherhood is a complicated thing. Being a daughter is a complicated thing.*

He met my gaze. I couldn't quite get over how strange it was to stare back into eyes that mirrored my own. "I got all your letters."

"When?"

"What?"

"When did you get the letters?" I pressed.

"About a year ago."

I frowned. "I sent the first one over three years ago. You're a little late."

"I know." His pale eyes widened in the same way mine do when I'm trying to cultivate sympathy. I looked away.

"But you have to understand—"

I interrupted him. "I don't have to do anything."

"Whoa." He leaned back into the couch and put his hands up. "You have your mother's temper."

"How would you know?"

"Taliah," he said softly. "I love that name, by the way."

My skin felt itchy, like it was suddenly three sizes too small. "It was Mom's grandma's name."

"I know."

I heard a beeping sound and turned toward the kitchen.

"Oh!" Harlow said, jumping up from the chair. "That's the cupcakes. I'm going to . . ." She trailed off and slinked

25

away to the kitchen. Leaving me alone with Julian Oliver.

"I can't believe it took you this long," I said slowly.

"I know, and I can't offer you any good excuses." He stared at his hands. He had prominent knuckles. That was something I'd noticed one late night when I was Googling him and had zoomed in on one of the famous photographs that Annie Leibovitz had taken of him. "But in my defense, I didn't even know your letters existed until a year ago."

"So you say."

"It's the truth. The girl who . . ." He fidgeted on the couch.

"It's okay. It's not like I'm naive enough to think that people like you sit around all day reading letters from all the random people that adore you." I realized my tone was bitter, but hell, I think I had the right to be bitter.

"People like me?"

"Famous people."

He blanched. "It's not like that."

"Okay. Whatever you say."

He nodded quickly. Another nervous tic. "So. As I was saying, the girl who reads the mail, she began to notice that we were getting a lot of letters from you. And she brought the letters to Mikey."

"Mikey?"

"Our manager."

I nodded. That's right. I'd come across that name in my online sleuthing.

"And Mikey, of course, recognized the last name."

"Mikey knew my mother?"

Julian bobbed his head quickly in agreement. "Oh yeah. Mikey grew up in Oak Falls with me. I used to work for his dad. He was there the day I met your mother. Heck, he was there for everything."

"Everything," I said. Something about the infiniteness of that word made me feel sad. And lonely. Mikey may have been around for everything, but I surely had not been. And no one had even bothered to give me the SparkNotes.

His eyes softened and I noticed he had a ring of green around his irises that I didn't possess. "Yes, everything. And now that I'm here, Taliah, I want to share everything with you."

I could feel my resolve fading, my anger giving way to melancholy. I crossed my arms. "Then why did it take you a year to get here?"

"I called Lena." His eyes locked with mine. "I mean, your mother."

Lena. It was unbelievably odd to hear that name coming out of his mouth. "What happened when you called her?"

He cleared his throat. "Well, I called her multiple times, actually."

"Dude. This isn't Little League softball or something. You don't get points for participation."

He gave me a small, sad smile. "I know."

"But what did Mom say?"

"She demanded that I stay away."

"Stay away," I repeated. That was a finely tuned euphemism if I'd ever heard one.

"Yes. She begged me not to answer your letters. Not to call you. And certainly not to try and see you."

I gripped the armrest of the chair that Harlow had recently vacated. "And you listened to her?"

"I felt like I had to. I owed her that at least." Something crossed over his face. Guilt. Or maybe regret.

I could feel my face flushing with heat. "Why? Don't you think I should have had some say in that decision?"

He was silent. I pressed, "Don't you?"

He hung his head and stared at the woven carpet, a braided mix of teals and grays. Another item Mom and I had selected from the Anthro catalog a few years ago when we decided to redecorate most of the house to celebrate her promotion to the Dr. Jefferson Reynolds Chair of Art History at Bellwether University. This was a few months before my discovery of The Shoebox.

"Don't you?" I said for the third time.

"Of course I do. That's why I'm here now."

"Three years too late." *Sixteen years too late.*

"Haven't you ever heard of better late than never?" he said in a sheepish tone.

I looked away.

"I was kidding," he added.

"I know," I said. "I just didn't find it that funny."

He let out a loud, awkward whistling sound. "Fair enough. But I'm here now. So can we at least . . ." He trailed off.

"At least?"

"At least talk. I want to get to know you."

I cocked my eyebrows in a dramatic fashion. "Well, that's a tall order, Mr. Oliver."

He groaned. "Please don't call me that."

"I'm not going to call you 'Dad.'" The word "Dad" left a bitter taste in my mouth. Like black coffee or dark chocolate—something that tasted a bit off now, but I knew I could learn to like if I worked at it. I swallowed a few times.

"Of course," he said. "I'm not asking you to. Just, please don't call me Mr. Oliver. Mr. Oliver is . . ." He paused. "My father."

"Right," I said, and suddenly felt like a huge asshat.

"The one who's dying."

"I'm sorry," I said, because I didn't know what else to say. "Sorry" was a free pass of a word. It cost nothing and bought you time.

"I wish you could've met him when he still had his wits about him."

Something inside me stirred and I sank down into the white leather chair. Mom was a big fan of the type of furniture that envelops you and swallows you whole.

"It's a big regret of mine," he continued. "The second I found out about you, I should've fought harder. I should've begged Lena to let me introduce you to my family. Taliah—" He paused again. "Can I call you that?"

I nodded.

"You have a family in Oak Falls, Taliah. They would love to get to know you." He tapped his fingers against his leg. I'd watched so many videos of him playing the guitar with those fingers. "They deserve to get to know you."

"Like how I deserved to get to know you?"

"Yes."

I stood back up. I brushed my hands against my acid-wash jeans, pressing out imaginary wrinkles. "I just don't get why you're here now."

A loud clanking sound came from the kitchen. Then a rustling, and Harlow poked her head into the living room. "Sorry about that. Ignore me." Before I could beg her to stay with us, she scurried back into the sanctuary of the kitchen.

"My father is dying," he said, his voice registering in a lower octave than before. It reminded me of the tonal quality he used to sing "Your Life in the Rain," one of his band's most popular songs. It was supposed to inspire the listener to feel nostalgic and melancholy. But it usually made me feel furious.

How dare you try to break my heart? I'd want to scream when listening to the track. *You don't have the right.*

"Your grandfather," he added as if he wasn't sure I would be able to piece together the connection. "And I don't know." He sighed and tugged at his hair. "The whole thing has really done a number on me."

"Right," I said softly. "Like, let me guess? It made you realize how fast life goes. Made you want to focus on what really matters."

"Goddamn. You remind me so much of your mother. That biting wit."

I shrugged. "She did raise me."

"Taliah," he said slowly, stretching my name out like it was something to savor. "I don't want to fight with you."

"I didn't realize we were fighting."

"You know what I mean."

I didn't say anything. I focused on a framed photograph of Mom holding nine-year-old me on her shoulders on a trip we'd taken to Cambridge. We were dressed in matching ruby red wool sweaters. I was wearing a funny-looking brown corduroy beret. She'd been invited to give a series of lectures at Harvard on Ed Ruscha. It was a big deal, I remember, because she'd recently finished up her doctorate and this was one of the first prestigious speaking engagements she'd landed.

When I was first born, Mom had been a working artist. She'd actually had some of her sculptures shown at a few prominent galleries in New York. The showings had even garnered some favorable write-ups in big-time publications like the *Village Voice*. But before I turned two, she'd enrolled in graduate school with the intention of earning her doctorate. And ever since she'd earned it, she hadn't publicly shown her artwork. Not once.

I studied the photograph some more and zeroed in on her knowing wide brown eyes. I wondered what she would think of the situation currently unfolding in our living room.

I felt like a traitor.

I felt impossibly angry at her.

And I felt confused. My heart pulling me in one direction, my head pulling me in the other. There was a tectonic shift happening inside of me.

"I'm just going to come out and say it," Julian announced. "That's one thing I've learned over the years. To be direct."

I frowned. That seemed like such a flimsy thing to have taken away from years of experience in the music industry. But I was curious, so I turned my attention from the photograph and back to him. "Okay."

"I know this is a pretty wild and crazy idea, but I want you to come with me to meet your grandfather before he passes."

I blinked. "What?"

"You heard me. I want you to come to Oak Falls with me right now. It'll be a short trip. But it will give us a chance to get to know one another. And a chance for you to meet your aunts, cousins, and grandmother. And of course, your grandfather."

I'd frequently fantasized about meeting my father. Even before I had the slightest inkling that my father was Julian Oliver. But my fantasies had never included the extended family that was likely to come with discovering the other half of me. Maybe that thought had never crossed my mind because most all of Mom's extended family lived in Jordan. Or maybe my brain had never processed the fact that of course, even rock stars have mothers and fathers and siblings.

He broke the uncomfortable silence with a question. "Do you play?"

"What?" I said, startled. I followed Julian's eyes to the piano that sat near the bay window in the living room.

"Oh. Yeah. But you know that."

"Huh?"

"I wrote about that in my letters to you."

In several of my letters to Julian, I'd mentioned that I played the piano. What I hadn't mentioned, at least not directly, were my own musical ambitions. I loved writing songs. Since I was seven, I could remember hearing various melodies in my head or coming up with an interesting phrase, and then jotting it down in my journal. I'd spend days, months, years fiddling with those melodies and snippets—I loved the puzzle of songs. The rewarding feeling of placing all the pieces in just the right order.

But when I'd started to suspect that Julian Oliver was my father, I felt a slight panic. Sure, my own interest in music was just one more thing that made my suspicions seem more like truth than fiction, but I felt like a copycat. I hadn't wanted to tell him about my own songwriting in case he would mistakenly think I wanted something from him. Which I didn't. Or at least not like that.

What I'd wanted were answers.

He tapped his fingers against his leg again. "The piano. Of course. I remember that now. But it was a huge fight with Lena, right?"

I pinched my lips together. "A struggle for sure. She's always been suspicious of my interest in music. I guess now I understand why."

"Will you play something for me?"

I locked eyes with him. It was like staring at a fun-house version of myself. There was something so familiar about those eyes, but also something so alien. "You have a lot of nerve, you know that?"

"Yes," he said plainly. "I do."

"To come in here after years of absence and just start

making all these requests," I continued.

He grinned a little. "Well, I thought maybe you could play something for me while you thought about my other request."

I considered this. "Okay. Fine."

I knew I should've been nervous. It wasn't every day that I was asked to play the piano for a full-fledged rock star. I mean, this dude was the recipient of a Grammy Award. Responsible for a multiplatinum album. But somehow, I wasn't that nervous. The idea of playing the piano actually felt calming. Looking back, I'm sure this was some sort of mind trick on his part. He probably knew it would be calming because we shared half of the same genetics, and playing music was obviously cathartic for him.

Also, despite Julian Oliver's frightening level of fame, there was no way he was as impossibly intimidating as my current piano teacher, a wrinkle-faced German man named Bruno—the most swelling praise I'd ever received from Bruno was "That didn't make me want to claw my eyes out." So there you have it. If I wrote for *Rolling Stone*, the headline of this moment would've been: "Julian Oliver Is No Bruno Kaufman."

He was silent and still while I made my way to the piano. I slid my legs up onto the bench and scooted to find a comfortable seat. My fingers hovered above the keys as I contemplated what song I should play.

I knew Julian Oliver would want—would expect—me to play some rock anthem. Something that would confirm that I was his effortlessly cool offspring. But unfortunately, even if I wanted to play a rock ballad, my repertoire was severely limited.

It's not like Bruno was teaching me how to play Nirvana or Radiohead or the Black Lips. Let alone something edgier or less mainstream. Bruno was sort of a strictly Bach and Rachmaninoff guy. And Mom followed Bruno's suit, so she flipped if she ever heard me playing something that you wouldn't hear lightly pouring out of the speakers at a fancy French restaurant. Of course I broke Mom's rules and tinkered around behind Bruno's back—loosely teaching myself how to play a handful of angry rock goddess songs—but none of my self-taught melodies seemed right for this moment.

I pressed down on the keys and began to play "Feeling Good." I'd played the song so many times that my muscle memory basically took over. My fingers splayed out, moving back and forth almost as if an invisible puppeteer were controlling them.

For my fourteenth birthday, Mom had purchased the sheet music for me. It was a big deal that she brought music into our home that wasn't classical. Yes, that's right. To Mom, even Nina Simone was a stretch.

As I played the song, I smiled to myself thinking of the

irony of the lyrics. I hummed under my breath. I loved how the song continued to build underneath my fingers. It felt like tossing gasoline on a fire. It literally smoldered. It made me feel powerful when I played it.

When I finished, I turned around to face Julian. He was beaming, but there was something off about it. There was an artificial brightness to him—his face was not a cloudless sky, but more like a fluorescent lightbulb.

He clapped once. "Bravo."

I narrowed my eyes at him. "That's not exactly the reaction I was expecting."

"What? I think you're a really talented pianist."

"But . . . ?"

"No but."

"Yes there is. I can tell there is most definitely a capital-*B* But. Just tell me."

He wrinkled his nose. "Nina Simone. Really?"

"What's wrong with Nina Simone? She's a goddess. And it's a classic."

"It's . . ." He stretched his legs out in front of him, dragging his heels along the woven carpet.

"It's what? One of the most perfect songs in the entirety of the universe?"

He frowned teasingly. "You can't really think that."

"You can't really think that it's not."

"It's stuffy," he argued.

"No way! It's sophisticated."

"Jesus." He shook his head. "Lena raised you to be a snob. I should've figured."

"'Raised' being the key word," I said, not missing a beat.

He bristled. "I guess I walked right into that one."

I nodded. "It's not exactly like you were around to show me the dark side."

He arched an eyebrow. "Yeah. If only I'd been able to supply you with *Nevermind* and *Loose Nut* and *Goo*."

I played along. "If only. Maybe I would've even been cool enough to own *White Light/White Heat* on vinyl."

His face lit up. "You are my daughter."

I shrugged and stared at the woven carpet. If you looked at it long enough without blinking, the blues all started to run together.

"That's kind of typical, though, isn't it?" I finally said.

"What?"

"That you, as a white dude, decide to disparage the music of a black woman by calling it 'stuffy.'"

The color drained from his face. "You know I didn't mean it like that." He squirmed as I stared at him. "You can't possibly think . . . I mean, your mother."

"My mother?"

"Well, you can't think I'm, you know, prejudiced. You have to know . . ."

I felt my whole body stiffen with discomfort. "Because

38

you slept with my mother to create me and she isn't white, you think that somehow adds up to you not being 'you know, prejudiced'?"

"Jesus!" he exclaimed again. He shoved a hand through his messy hair and shook his head. The wrinkles at the corners of his eyes suddenly seemed more pronounced. For a brief moment, a sadness welled in me. I'd never seen him, known him without those wrinkles. He'd had lifetimes before this moment.

I'd missed out on lifetimes.

"Taliah," he said, clearly trying to keep his voice calm. "I just don't like that song. It's not my type of music."

"Okay," I said.

"I know you're angry with me. And you want to pick fights. But please."

I shrugged. "I was just making an observation."

A few long beats of silence.

"Come home with me," he said. "It'll give you the chance to make many more observations. And for me to hopefully redeem myself in some small way."

"I am home."

"You know what I mean."

I glanced up. He was looking at me expectantly with those freakishly familiar eyes.

"Please," he said. "We can spend the drive there fighting about music."

"I don't want to fight with you."

"You know what I mean," he repeated.

"You keep saying that. But I'm not sure I do 'know what you mean,' dude." I didn't mean to be so petulant, but I kept hearing my mother's voice in my head.

"Be careful before you trust people, Taliah," she would say. She's an extremely guarded person, and I never quite understood why she put up such thick and tall walls. Part of me always wondered if it had to do with my absent dad, and the fact she'd unexpectedly gotten pregnant with me. Now, knowing about Julian, I wondered even more if it had something to do with how things had gone down in their relationship. Had he given her a reason to be so guarded?

I also think it had something to do with her being an immigrant. And an Arab, Muslim immigrant at that. Given the cultural climate, which only seemed to be growing more hostile, she protected herself and me by never divulging too much about herself to strangers or random acquaintances. But the problem with this strategy, as I knew all too well since Harlow was my only close friend, was that those random acquaintances never had the chance to develop into anything else. I understood why Mom always wanted to be cautious, but sometimes I wondered what that cost us.

"Sorry," I said, staring at his face, which looked a little wounded. "I know I'm being difficult. It's just this is . . . difficult."

"I know," he said sympathetically. "I understand." He leaned forward, pressing his elbows against his knees. It was a childish posture for a man of his age to take, and that seemed fitting somehow. "Please come with me."

"Mom would flip."

"I want her to come too."

"That's going to be a little tough."

He nodded in agreement. "But I think I can convince her."

I paused for a moment and briefly enjoyed my position of possessing information that he clearly did not have. He seemed so confident. Like he knew that he had some sort of unearthly, magical pull over my mother. I wondered whether this magnetic confidence was a product of being a rock star, or the reason he had been able to become one. "Can you teleport her from Paris?"

He coughed and straightened his spine. "Paris?"

"Yeah. She's currently in Paris."

He exhaled. "Wow. Okay. I didn't exactly expect that."

"So does that mess up everything?" A sudden feeling of disappointment gripped me. I was worried he was just going to get up and leave.

He shook his head. "Not busted. Just different." His face was blank and then a smile washed over it. "Maybe this is actually better."

"What is?"

"You can come now without her permission. When does she get back?"

I momentarily thought about lying and then decided against it. "Sunday."

His face scrunched up. "She left you alone for this long?"

I shrugged. "What's wrong with that? Besides, she invited me. But I wanted to stay home."

His eyes darted around the living room. "You wanted to stay here instead of going to Paris?"

"Yes."

He smiled slightly. "Oh. That's right. You are *sixteen*."

I groaned. "Really? You're going to mock me now?"

He quickly backpedaled. "Sorry, sorry." His eyes met mine and he lowered his voice to that famous low-register octave of his. "Please come, Taliah."

"Would you excuse me for a second?" I stood up from the chair. "I need a cupcake."

Dear Julian Oliver,

I have to admit I'm a little surprised that I haven't heard from you yet. Part of me really thought you would come rushing to meet me.

I'm choosing to give you the benefit of the doubt that my first letter got lost in the enormous pile of fan mail that you must receive on a weekly basis. So my new plan is to write you over and over again in the hopes that one of these letters will catch the eye of a curious intern and find its way to you. (You do have an intern, right? It seems like all famous people have assistants and those assistants in turn have interns.)

I thought you should know I worked up the nerve to ask Mom about it. And guess what? Her face drained of color. I could tell she was about to start crying. And I can count on one hand the number of times I have ever seen her cry. She said she wanted to tell me about this one day, but that she wasn't ready yet. And that my father was no longer in our lives for a good reason.

But I don't believe her.

I've attached a photograph of me smiling so you can see the resemblance between us. I'll give you that I probably look more like Mom than I look like you, but look at my eyes. Don't you see it? And the way my lips curve? I think we have a similarly shaped mouth. I hope that isn't a weird thing to say. Okay, maybe it is a weird thing to say. But dude, I don't think you are in the position to judge me for being weird.

Anyway, I have to go. I have a science report due tomorrow on the bubonic plague. Did you know that in the late Middle Ages, the bubonic plague wiped out one-third of the entire human population? Imagine that. And not to guilt-trip you or anything, but all the scientists are predicting we are due for another insane disease outbreak, and I'd sort of like to meet you before that happens.

Write me back soon?

Your maybe-possibly-probably daughter,
Taliah Sahar Abdallat

P.S. I've been doing some research on the illegitimate daughters of rock stars. (FWIW, I hate the word "illegitimate." It makes me feel icky, but I'll use it for now.) In my research, I came across the story of Liv Tyler and Steven Tyler, and it'd be pretty great if you could hook me up with a role in some blockbuster fantasy series. I have slightly pointy ears, so I might make a good elf.

P.P.S. I'm not sure if I get my ear shape from you. It's hard to find a good photo of your ears.

V.

I found Harlow in the kitchen. She was sitting on one of the elevated wooden stools at the breakfast bar, devouring a freshly baked pistachio cupcake, jamming out to something on her iPhone. When she caught sight of me, she slipped off her earbuds and pushed the tray of cupcakes toward me. "Want one?"

I sat down beside her and grabbed a cupcake. I took a large bite. The nutty pistachio taste mixed with the sweet buttercream of the icing. Perfection. "These are so freaking good."

"I know," Harlow said brightly.

"Is Quinn still thinking about renaming her band Cupcakes on Crack in your honor?"

The tips of Harlow's ears reddened. Harlow never blushed in her cheeks. Only in her ears. "I think so." She tapped her fingers against the rose-colored quartz of the breakfast bar. Her black fingernail polish was starting to chip. "But why are we talking about that when"—she thumbed toward the living room—"this is happening?"

I shrugged. "I dunno. That"—I imitated her thumbing gesture—"is way overwhelming. Plus, I was trying to seem interested."

Harlow sometimes accused me of not being *interested* or *invested* in anything that had to do with Quinn. To be honest, Quinn's band was still a bit of a sore subject between Harlow and me. Before Quinn, Harlow and I had been toying around with a music project. I don't know if you could call it a band exactly.

I wrote the music. And the two of us came up with lyrics, and then Harlow sang them while I played the piano. It was sort of jazzy—sort of cabaret with a punk edge. We would go to the thrift store and find ridiculous outfits to wear while performing—vintage dresses and pumps, leopard-print boas, cloche hats.

We never performed for anyone except ourselves, and accidentally my mother a few times. But we'd had plans to maybe enter our school's talent show or a local battle of the bands competition. But then Harlow met Quinn. And Quinn was the lead singer in a newly formed band. A real band. One that performed at real venues and had a real, if small, fan base.

Harlow suddenly seemed embarrassed of our little project. She started making excuses about why she didn't have time to practice and kept dodging my invitations to come over and brainstorm lyrics to a new melody I'd come up with. I quickly got the message and dropped it. I've never been good at confronting people. Especially when I'm afraid of the answer.

On the afternoons when Harlow was busy hanging out with Quinn and Quinn's friends, I sometimes would take out one of the vintage costumes we'd found at the thrift store, put it on, and play my heart out on the piano. That helped me to feel less lonely.

"I miss it," I blurted out.

"What?" said Harlow.

"Everything."

Harlow licked some of the frosting off her cupcake. She glanced down at her fingers. "I know. Me too."

"Do you?" I pressed.

She nodded, and somehow that was enough for now.

I fiddled with the wrapper on my cupcake. "He wants me to go to Oak Falls with him."

"I know. I overheard."

I gave her a questioning look and pointed at the earbuds.

"They aren't completely noise-canceling," she said sheepishly.

I dipped my finger into the icing and licked it. "You've been eavesdropping?"

"Obviously. I mean, I know he's your dad. Or maybe your dad. But he was Julian Oliver first. That's kind of a big freaking deal."

I laughed a little. "Yeah. I guess it is a big freaking deal. So should I go?"

She sighed. "Honestly, Tal. I don't know. I have a million questions. Like I'm sure you do."

I set my half-eaten cupcake to the side and rested my elbows against the kitchen counter. "Yeah. But maybe this is my chance to get answers."

Harlow touched my wrist. "Don't you think you should at least call your mom?"

"She'd flip out."

"Exactly."

"But what if she's flipping out for the wrong reasons?"

Harlow took her hand away and leaned back so she could study me. "What do you mean?"

"Maybe the situation between them is complicated. I guess I've built up this big narrative in my head that he's"—I thumbed toward the living room again—"this big asshole that left her. And maybe that's true. But maybe it isn't. The truth of it is that I don't know anything."

"Right. But—"

I cut her off. "And don't you think it's more than a little weird that she's kept this from me my entire life?"

"Yeah. But I'm sure she has her reasons. I trust your mom. What I don't know is if we can trust *him*."

I grabbed the cupcake and took another bite. "It's not like he's going to ax-murder me or something."

"Right." Harlow looked for a moment like she was actually considering the likelihood of that. "I'd sure hope not. But there are a million other dangers involved in going off on a trip with a strange man besides getting ax-murdered."

"Is he a strange man?"

"Yes," Harlow said emphatically. "I know you think he's your—"

"He's already admitted he is!"

"Yeah," Harlow pointed out. "He's admitted it, but your mom has never told you that."

"Exactly. And isn't that fucked up? For fuck's sake, she told me my dad was *dead*. Dead, Harlow. That's a pretty traumatic thing to tell a little girl, especially if it isn't true."

"Maybe," Harlow said slowly.

"Harlow. Come on."

"Okay. It's pretty messed up. But only if he is, in fact, your father. And we don't know that for sure."

"Should I demand we get a DNA test right now? Should I

march in there and swab out some of his saliva?"

She rolled her eyes, exasperated. "I wasn't saying that."

"So what were you saying?"

"That you should call your mom."

"But she's going to tell me not to go."

"Exactly."

We stared at each other for a few moments.

"So I have an idea," I finally said.

"Taliah," she groaned. "Please. Not one of your ideas."

"Hear me out."

She licked frosting off her thumbnail.

"Why don't you and I both go with him to Oak Falls."

"Taliah," she repeated sternly.

"And that way, you'll know I'm safe."

She frowned. "It doesn't work like that. Plus, I made plans with Quinn tonight."

I matched her frown. "You can reschedule with Quinn."

Harlow gave me a helpless look. "I just don't know, Tal."

"Okay. How about you think about it this way? Push everything else aside and focus on the fact that Julian Oliver, famous front man of an iconic rock band, is sitting in my living room asking us to take a road trip with him. Forget the other details. You'd say yes to that."

"Asking you."

"Semantics," I said.

"Road trip to Oak Falls, Indiana."

"So?" I said, and repeated, "Semantics."

"I don't think that word means what you think it means."

"Semantics," I said, a big stupid grin spreading across my face. "Come on, Har. This summer has been so boring so far. Let's do something fun."

She frowned again. "I don't think it's been boring."

I groaned. "That's because you have a hot girlfriend. But me? Not so much action happening."

Harlow made a face.

"I'm kidding. But seriously, come on. Let's do something memorable. Me and you."

"And him," Harlow said, glancing toward the living room.

"Yeah. And him. The famous freaking rock star."

"That we don't know."

"Right. Which is the point of the aforementioned trip," I argued. "Plus," I added, hoping to play to Harlow's sentimental side, "it will give me a chance to meet my grandparents. I've never met any of my grandparents."

Harlow looked uncertain. "That's because they still live in Jordan."

"Lived," I corrected her. "Mom's dad died before she even came to the US. Her mom died a few years later."

"Right."

"So this would be really special. It's a chance to meet my grandfather before he passes." I watched her facial features

51

wrinkle in thought. "And to meet my grandma. Maybe she's really cool. Maybe I could actually forge a relationship with one of my four grandparents. Twenty-five percent isn't great, but it's something."

Harlow took a deep breath, pulled out her phone, and texted something quickly. I could tell she was softening.

"And," I continued, piling it on, "this is my chance to really learn what went down with my parents, you know? This is my history, Harlow. Don't you think I deserve to know it?"

Her eyebrows knitted together, her eyes still glued to her phone screen.

"Is that a yes?" I pressed.

"Okay, fine. But when we get there, you call your mom."

I grinned. "Deal."

VI.

I didn't pack anything. Only the clothes I was wearing—a long-sleeve striped T-shirt, my acid-wash jeans, and red Converses. In retrospect, packing nothing other than the clothes I was wearing was probably a poor choice, but I wanted to get on the road before Harlow had a chance to change her mind.

Apparently all of my previous adolescent fantasies had been correct when I'd pictured Julian driving up to our house in a vintage Mustang convertible with a throaty, rumbling engine, because I presently found myself in the backseat of such a car. Though, in fairness, I bet that I'd read about his car in one of the zillions of articles on him I'd devoured when I became convinced he was my dad, and that tidbit must've wedged its way into my brain.

Outside the car window, my neighborhood was a blur of brick houses, anemic newly planted trees, and perfectly manicured green lawns. My subdivision features four models of houses that alternate block by block in an almost eerily Stepfordish pattern. Seriously, I know Arcade Fire wrote *The Suburbs* about their neighborhood in Houston, but that record could definitely have been written about my town. To answer Win Butler's question: It is impossible to escape the sprawl when it comes to Chester, Ohio.

It's a bummer, actually, because the area closer to Bellwether University, where Mom works, is much more hip. It's full of slanted old Victorian houses that press right up against natural food markets and used-book stores. But Mom insisted on buying a home in the suburbs because of the way elementary school zoning worked.

Before we'd fully exited the cookie-cutter streets of my subdivision, Julian requested that I put on some music. And much to his chagrin, I'd chosen the *Hamilton* soundtrack.

"This is really what the kids are listening to these days?" he asked.

"Yes!" I said, and Harlow added, "It actually is. I don't even like Broadway musicals and I love *Hamilton*. Lin-Manuel Miranda is a genius."

"What makes it so genius?" Julian asked, shouting so that we could hear him over Daveed Diggs's rapping.

"SO. MANY. THINGS," Harlow and I said in unison.

"Like?" he prompted.

"Well, for starters, the diverse cast and the mixing of hip-hop music with more classical Broadway ballads help reclaim this central piece of American history for those of us who might not have previously felt like it was ours," I explained. "I want to someday write a show like *Hamilton*. One that inspires brown girls to claim their due."

"Wow," Julian said. "Very cool. Though I'm sure this won't come as a big surprise to you or anything, I know jack shit about musicals." I saw his face twist up in the rearview mirror, his lips puckered like he'd just bit into a fresh lemon. "But my God. My child wants to write musicals. Like we're talking about the same thing, right? Singing-dancing plays?"

"Yup," I said cheerfully.

"She's kind of a nerd," Harlow said, nudging her shoulder against mine. "But Tal, be honest. You don't want to just write musicals. You also write songs."

Julian's eyebrows shot up. "You write songs?"

I was miffed. It wasn't Harlow's place to reveal that. I felt safe offering the tidbit about musicals because that was something I'd thought about wanting to do way far off in the future. The way I sometimes thought about wanting to hike the Inca trail or visit the Galapagos Islands. It wasn't

55

concrete. It wasn't yet personal to me the way that songs I wrote with Harlow were.

I nodded silently, and Harlow added, "Yeah. She composes songs on the piano and the two of us come up with lyrics." She looked at me eagerly, clearly oblivious to my irritation, and then exclaimed, "We should perform one of our songs for Julian!"

I shook my head. "We don't do that anymore."

Julian looked at us through the rearview mirror. "What do you mean?"

I shrugged and stared down at my sneakers. "We don't write songs anymore."

"Why not?"

Neither Harlow nor I said anything.

Julian cleared his throat, fully aware he'd waded into awkward territory. I thought he would press me more about my songwriting, but I was relieved when he let it go. "I don't know what makes me feel weirder," he joked. "That I'm old enough to have a sixteen-year-old daughter or that I'm relying on that daughter to let me know what the kids are listening to these days. I used to be the kid, ya know? Shit, I'm old." Julian nervously glanced at us. "And I feel like a chaperone. An old-ass chaperone."

"I think you mean chauffeur," Harlow corrected, not looking up from her cell phone, where she was texting Quinn.

The highway spit out in front of us. Flat and gray and

framed by expanses of cornfields that stretched as far as the eye could see. The late midday light streamed into the car, a hazy pink, and it made me feel sentimental and foggy, like this moment was already a memory and I was just living inside it.

Julian must've seen something on my face because he asked, "You okay, kid?"

I pressed my lips together and nodded.

"You don't have to be nervous. My folks—" And then he corrected, "your folks. They're your folks, too." He shot me a worried look. I hadn't been that nervous and now I suddenly was.

"Don't be nervous," he repeated. "They'll be ecstatic to meet you."

"Do they know we're coming?" Harlow asked, not looking up from her phone.

I was slightly annoyed that Harlow felt comfortable enough to take charge of the conversation. To ask questions and insert herself without any shred of discomfort. But that was Harlow. Her parents, like my mother, were professors at Bellwether University. While my mother was the reserved, serious type of professor who dressed mostly in all black and was constantly carrying a café latte, Harlow's parents were the classic bohemian-style professors. They regularly served Tofurky and kombucha at dinner and always encouraged Harlow to speak her mind, teaching her that there wasn't a single topic of conversation that was off-limits. This led to Harlow being the type of person who had never encountered a situation where she wasn't immediately chatty and unguarded.

I guess you could say Harlow and I were opposites in that way. And usually I was fine to let her do the talking, but this situation felt different.

"Why? Who's asking?" Julian joked.

Harlow didn't respond. She was completely sucked into her phone.

Julian cleared his throat again with a cough. The action of someone who was not used to being ignored. "Who are you texting?" Julian's tone was light, but it reeked of adult desperation. I was embarrassed for him and I squirmed in my seat. "Your boyfriend?" Julian continued to tease. I cringed and stared down at my ragged fingernails.

"Girlfriend," Harlow snapped.

"Oh," Julian said.

"Oh?" Harlow looked up from her phone.

"Nothing," Julian said. "Good for you."

"Good for me?" Harlow let out a fake laugh. "You're such the prototypical middle-aged white dude."

"Whoa!" He tapped his fingers against the steering wheel. "Shots fired."

"I'm calling it how I see it," she answered, and gazed pointedly out the window. The fading sunlight glinted against her nose ring, which was new. Quinn had talked her into it. And as much as I wanted to begrudge it because it was yet another New Thing That Came from Quinn, the piercing suited Harlow. It gave her a glamorous edge.

But as I watched her, my feelings of affection slowly slipped to anger. It was strange—I'd felt totally fine ragging on him about his reaction to the Nina Simone song, silently judging his desperation vying for attention moments ago, but listening to Harlow lay into him made me irritated. He was my dad to judge and criticize. Not hers. Though I couldn't really argue with her—he was pretty much the definition of a middle-aged white dude, albeit with the black skinny jeans.

"Kids these days," Julian said. "You guys are all language police."

"Just because we want the world to be more equitable and less oppressive doesn't make us the 'language police,'" Harlow said.

"Yeah, but if you're constantly outraged about everything, how will you ever know when to be really upset? How will you know when something is really worth fighting for?"

"I think I'll manage," Harlow whispered in the way she only did when she was actually very pissed off.

I pondered Julian's question for a moment, and I wasn't really sure. I was used to feeling lots of things, but I still hadn't learned how to categorize and weigh them. That felt like a task I would master years later when I was forced to wear a tweed skirt and cream-colored pumps to my office job. As far as I was concerned, my job at sixteen was to feel things. To really feel them.

And feeling seemed good enough for now.

"I think you'd really like Harlow's girlfriend's band," I said, trying to broker a peace offering between the two of them. But really maybe I was trying to broker a peace offering between Harlow and me. I wanted to fix whatever was broken between us, but the problem was I didn't know how to fix something that neither of us had admitted was broken. "Really?" Julian said. "I'd like to hear it. But I'd also like to hear one of your songs."

I ignored his last comment and turned to Harlow. "Put on one of Quinn's songs."

Harlow looked at me nervously. A few moments ago, she had been all bravado, triumphantly calling Julian out on all of his failings and microaggressions, and now the tips of her ears were turning red and she was nervously flipping her phone back and forth between her palms. "I don't know. He probably isn't interested in hearing it."

"Wait. Is it another Broadway tune?" Julian asked.

"Hell no," Harlow said quickly. And then she looked at me and added, "Not that there's anything wrong with that."

"You guys are lame. *Hamilton* is a true masterpiece," I groaned.

"You're right. And you know I like it, okay. But I'd still

rather listen to 'Kiss Off' over and over again than hear George Washington rap," Harlow said.

I rolled my eyes as Julian exclaimed, *"Yes!"* and raised his hand and tapped the car's ceiling excitedly. He craned his neck back to flash Harlow a grin. "The Violent Femmes are the very best." He stuck his hand out to high-five her. "Now you're giving me some hope for the future of the youth of this country."

"'I hope you know this will go down on your permanent record,'" Harlow sneered-sang.

"'Oh, yeah? Well, don't get so distressed/Did I happen to mention that I'm impressed?'" Julian sang back.

I was already starting to feel like a third wheel on a date when Julian peered back at Harlow and said, "You sure things aren't mixed up and you're not actually the one who's my daughter?"

Harlow's eyes shot straight to the floor mats. The whole car went silent. It was much too soon for that type of joke. Julian coughed awkwardly in what I assumed was an attempt to recover.

"Sooooo," he breathed out, "do you want to put on some of your girl's jams or what?"

Harlow glanced at me as if asking, *Is that okay? Or do we hate him now? Should I ice him out?* Loyalty. Despite everything that was broken between us, at least the two of us still had that.

61

I gave her a slight nod.

Harlow leaned forward and grabbed the auxiliary cord. She plugged her phone in and soon Quinn's tinny voice filled the car. I'd never found Quinn's band to be anything to write home about (or perhaps more accurately, to write Julian about), but Harlow loved them, of course. I briefly wondered if it was the same for Mom when she listened to S.I.T.A.'s songs. The thought made me feel queasy and guilty and I tried to chase it away.

Quinn's band is all slamming drums and squealing guitar chords. It's messy and capital-*L* Loud. I've gone with Harlow to a few shows, and I always stand out in the worst kind of way. I never know what to do with my hands or feet. Everyone else in their cheetah-print halter tops and red leather skirts seems to know exactly when to effortlessly move their hips or bob their head, and I end up feeling like I'm back in eighth grade at a bar mitzvah, fumbling my way through the Electric Slide. So yeah, I guess the polite way to put it is: I'm not the intended audience for Quinn's music. Though I do love the one song that Quinn sings that I think is about Harlow—"Cupcakes for Dinner."

Julian enthusiastically clapped his hands against the steering wheel. I didn't know him well enough to know if he genuinely was enjoying the music, or he just wanted to be kind. Regardless, I was glad he was kind. I sort of loved him for it. It was the first moment of the day where I felt something brew inside me, a recognition of something to admire about him that was deeper than his fame and celebrity.

"This is pretty good," he finally said.

I watched Harlow let out a shallow breath of relief. Her bravado returned. "I know. They're amazing."

In the rearview mirror, Julian flashed me a wry smile. A smile that had nothing to do with happiness, but everything to do with hope. A smile that said: *We are here now. Together. We should be happy. Please be happy.*

A wish of a smile.

I returned it, making a silent wish of my own, and then turned my eyes to the road unfurling before us.

"So," Harlow said after she'd turned off Quinn's band and switched to a vintage punk rock station curated by Google Music. Julian nodded his head along to a song with a sloppy bass line and tangled drumbeat. "Are you gonna tell us the story of you and Dr. Abdallat?"

In the rearview mirror, I watched Julian swallow. He stopped nodding his head along to the music. His face blanched.

"What do you mean?"

"You know exactly what I mean," Harlow continued. "How'd the two of you meet? Tell us all about your romantic courtship."

Her voice unnerved me. But more so, what she was asking unnerved me. I, of course, desperately wanted to know everything. Every tiny detail that made up my family history and, in only a slightly hyperbolic sense, made up the fiber of my very being.

I elbowed Harlow, which I had meant as a signal to knock it off, but instead it made her push it further. "And why did the two of you break up? There's got to be a juicy story there, right?"

I swallowed. That was the question that had been lurking in my brain since I'd discovered The Shoebox three years ago. The question that so much hinged on. *Why had Julian left? Had he not wanted me? Was he cruel to my mother? Worse, maybe, was she cruel to him?*

I desperately wanted my answer. Answers. But I also didn't. Because sometimes there is freedom in not knowing. You are able to fill in the blanks with whatever whimsical explanations you wish. You are able to cast the characters how you want, mold their motivations to your liking. You are in control of the narrative. You're not bound by cold and hard and possibly upsetting facts.

I expected Julian to shrug off Harlow. I didn't expect him to crack open so easily. But to my surprise, he drew a hand through his messy hair and said, "Okay. I guess I should start with when Lena landed in America."

Julian Oliver was going to fill in those blank spaces.

America was not what Lena had expected. Sure, as the plane had hovered above the tarmac, about to touch down in New York City, she'd spotted the landmarks she'd been primed to watch for—the Empire State Building, the Statue of Liberty, the various skyscrapers that burst from the ground like overgrown teeth. She couldn't stand looking at them for more than a few moments. They made her unreasonably nervous. And nauseous. The gravity-defying nature of the city unsettled her.

But her time in New York City had been a complete blur. A whirlwind through customs, where the shaggy-haired man had made her repeat everything at least three times. His hair color was one she'd never seen before—a bright orangish yellow. It reminded her of the sun back home in the late afternoon when it shone so brightly and whitened the whole sky.

"To study," she'd said. "At Hampton University in Indiana." She'd practiced saying "Indiana" many times before she'd boarded the flight from Amman, but now that the moment was here, the foreign, multisyllabic word stuck to her tongue like wax.

The customs officer had looked at her with confusion. She'd found this odd, as back in Jordan she'd been the top

English student in her class. She'd been praised for her authentic accent, her perfect pronunciation.

"Study what?" the officer had asked. He'd run his hand through his curiously colored hair.

"Medicine," she said. This is what she'd told her mother in their endless discussions of her plan to go to America to study. She'd known then that her only sliver of a chance of getting her mother to agree to her outrageous plan was to pledge an allegiance to a career as a doctor. That would be a source of family pride—her following in the footsteps of her father. As her father was dead, and he'd had no sons, this was a particularly compelling proposal.

And so her mother had finally acquiesced. But now, standing before the customs officer, Lena knew in her heart of hearts that she would never become a doctor. Something about that realization thrilled her. Something about that realization also terrified her and shamed her.

"And you have a student visa?"

Lena nodded, her tongue becoming waxier by the minute. She fumbled in her purse for the corresponding paperwork.

The whole ordeal was stilted and uncomfortable, but she'd made it past customs with her stamped passport and her single rolling suitcase with the ornery left wheel that always pulled to the right. And now she found herself riding in her cousin's husband's car, winding through grassy hills toward a town called Oak Falls. A place she couldn't even imagine, no matter how many hours she'd spent poring over the glossy brochure that Hampton University had sent to her from across the Atlantic Ocean.

She remembered the day that brochure had arrived. She'd held it in her hands as if the paper itself were made of magic. Her golden ticket.

She glanced out the window and had two distinct thoughts:

I've never seen so much green in my whole life.

I miss home.

The ache for home was palpable. It wasn't just a feeling. It was a physical thing that had taken up space in her stomach and was crawling its way up her chest.

"It'll fade," her cousin said, as if she'd read Lena's mind. She briefly looked over at her. Her cousin was sitting in the backseat with her while her husband drove them. "It will get easier. The first year is the hardest. If you can make it the first year, you will make it. If not, you can always return to Jordan."

She said the last sentence like it wasn't really an option. And of course, Lena knew it wasn't. She'd made her choice and now she had to make it a year.

She had to make it forever.

Once classes started, Lena began to understand that most of her fellow students lived on campus in small rooms all stacked next to one another. They even shared communal bathrooms, which she found to be a very strange custom. When her classmates asked her where she lived, they seemed to find her answer odd, as it was not a name like Bancroft or Wilton or Straton. But instead a simple address—21 May Street.

"Twenty-one May Street?" they would say, assuming that they had heard wrong, that Lena's answer had somehow gotten lost in translation. But no. She was uncertain about many things, but she knew she lived at 21 May Street.

She'd memorized that address. Spent hours practicing saying it in front of the mirror.

"Isn't that kind of, like, far from campus?" one girl with curly blond hair had asked.

"Yes," Lena had said, making sure to enunciate properly. She'd recently found that many of her English words seemed to get stuck in the base of her throat. She was trying her best not to swallow the words, not to silence her own voice. "It's by the hospital. I live with my cousin and her husband." Then Lena added, "He's a doctor."

The girl had politely nodded and then gone to sit with her other friends. Lena always sat in the middle row. Alone, always. She'd naively believed that her loneliness would subside once classes started, but if anything, the classes had made it worse. She was more aware than ever just how alone she was. How untethered.

Living with her cousin was *tolerable*. T-O-L-E-R-A-B-L-E. That was the best English word she could think of to describe the experience. It was not torturous nor was it pleasurable, but Lena was surviving. Her cousin had come to America with her husband, who was a doctor. He worked at Hampton University's teaching hospital. He was a pathologist who believed he should have been a surgeon. He was perplexed and somewhat dismissive of Lena's claims that she intended to become a doctor.

"Not a surgeon, though, correct?" he'd asked her one night as he helped himself to another serving of *bamieh*. He'd raised his caterpillar-like eyebrows in what she supposed he intended to be a jovial manner, but came off as slightly hostile and competitive.

She would've been more offended by this line of questioning if she actually believed she was destined to become a doctor.

Her cousin tried her best to make Lena feel at home. She made *mansaf* from scratch, driving miles out of town to find a grocery store that sold *halal* lamb and the right type of rice pilaf. Lena didn't have the heart to tell her that she couldn't have cared less if the lamb was *halal*, and that the *mansaf* only made her miss home more.

This particular afternoon, Lena had decided not to walk the two miles back home immediately after her last class let out. The air had begun to turn crisp and the leaves on the trees were turning the color of fire—a natural phenomenon she'd never experienced and was charmed by.

She pulled her jacket closer and followed a pack of students as they headed toward the main drag of campus. She browsed by the local shops and café, finally settling on an unremarkable-looking diner. She figured the menu would probably be easy enough to translate. She was still in the stage of trying at all costs to avoid embarrassing mix-ups.

A short girl wearing a red-checkered apron shouted at her from the back of the restaurant to sit anywhere she wanted. Lena glanced around the mostly empty room that was filled with metallic booths with sagging cushions and metallic tables with uncomfortable-looking chairs. The diner was less bright and lively than she'd thought it'd be. Disappointed, she slid into one of the ratty booths.

A menu for the restaurant, uncreatively named Oak Falls Diner, rested on the scratched metallic tabletop. She grabbed it and began to study it, slowly reviewing each choice aloud in her head.

Chili cheese dog, her mind sounded out. That sounded absolutely revolting.

Cheeseburger with fries. At least she knew what that was. But she hated the way Americans served their meat. Pink and raw, practically bloody.

Small garden salad. She looked at the picture accompanying this menu choice. It was the saddest-looking salad she had ever seen. Lettuce that somehow managed to be both pale and fluorescent at the same time, glistening in some sort of sauce.

Her menu perusing was interrupted by a voice. "So what will it be?"

When she looked up, she saw a man. He was dressed from head to toe in denim, a leather cuff on his left wrist. His hair was the color of uncooked corn, his eyes unnervingly blue. Something about those eyes reminded her of home, of her uncle's olive farm that sat on the rocky hills of Jabal Ajlun. In the winter months, she and her cousins would roam the windy hills and the sky would be a bright and impossibly clear blue. They would be able to see over the hills for miles and miles, which made them feel like little kings and queens.

"Sorry. Didn't mean to rush you," the man said, but he didn't take his blue eyes off her. "Do you need more time?"

She shook her head and took a deep breath before forcing herself to slowly say, "A cheeseburger with fries, please. Fully cooked, please." She silently cursed herself for saying "please" twice. She knew it would make her language sound stilted to American ears.

He cocked his head to study her more intensely, and not for the first time, she felt naked without her hijab. She had tossed it in a trash can at JFK, feeling slightly heartsick at the sight of the scarf that had once been her mother's—the scarf that her mother had tenderly wrapped around Lena's head before sending her off to the airport to fly across the ocean to America—floating to its graveyard, nestled between discarded candy bar wrappers and glossy tabloid magazines.

She hadn't tossed her hijab out of some strong personal conviction. She'd never felt oppressed by it. In Jordan, she didn't mind it at all. Actually, most of the time, she'd enjoyed wearing it. Sure, it was slightly uncomfortable, especially in the midday heat, but she mostly only wore it in public anyway. Never in her own house, as after her father passed it was only her, Aaliyah, and her mother.

So why had she tossed it? Well, she'd seen the way the customs officer had stared at it. She knew then that it marked her as different. And she did not want to be different in America. She wanted to be American, though she had no idea yet what that entailed. So yes, she'd tossed the headscarf. And every day since, she'd heard the ghost of her father chastising her for abandoning her identity so quickly for the sake of some perceived convenience. When she felt like defending herself, she would bitterly think that the hijab marked her as weak in the eyes of Americans, and she had not come to America to be weak.

She had come to change her life.

She had come to carve out a space for herself and fill it up without apology.

What she didn't realize then, but would come to realize many years later, is that she would spend the rest of her life making, searching for, and studying art that attempted to prove the very opposite—that it was not the hijab that had made her weak, but her willingness to so quickly shed an integral part of her identity. All the tiny write-ups in the *New York Times* and the *New Yorker* and the *Village Voice* that threw out words like "regret" and "nostalgia" would get close to understanding her purpose, but would never nail it. Her art would be and was an art of atonement. A reckoning of convenience versus belief. An exploration of the old immigrant adage of how much of yourself were you willing to destroy in order to melt into America.

But all of that would come later. For now, she was focused on the man who was openly studying her hair, which she'd admittedly spent a lot of time on that morning—brushing and then clipping back her bangs with a barrette. Her cousin, who still dutifully wore her hijab had watched her with interest, perhaps even judgment, not saying a word. As Lena studied this man, this strange man with the unnerving blue eyes, take in the soft waves of her brown mane, she felt an uncomfortable quickening in her pulse.

She instinctively reached out and touched her hair, tucking a few strands behind her ear.

"You sure you want the cheeseburger?" he said, and leaned in toward her in a conspiratorial manner. He lowered his voice and continued, "Between you and me, the cheeseburger here is not very good. Especially not if it's fully cooked. Though it's probably safer to eat that way, I'll give you that."

She turned away from his gaze as she felt her cheeks beginning to warm. "Is that so?"

"Yeah. Really nothing is that great here." His voice was still a hushed whisper. There was something intimate about that. "If you want a real solid cheeseburger, you should let me take you to Mickey's down on Trout Road."

She frowned at him and said the only thing that popped into her mind. "But I'm hungry now."

"Then let's go." He held out his hand, and she stared at it for a moment before taking it. He pulled her out of the booth and they walked out of the diner, hand in hand.

He didn't drop her hand once they exited the diner. This both terrified her and exhilarated her. They walked the hilly streets together, presumably headed toward Mickey's, him still holding firmly onto her hand.

"I've never been to Mickey's," she said finally.

"I figured."

She stopped walking and turned to look at him. "What do you mean by that?"

"Well," he said, a grin spreading across his face, "if you'd ever been to Mickey's, you wouldn't bother coming into the diner."

"Are you from here?"

His grin widened. "Guilty as charged. Born and bred, unfortunately. A townie. And you?"

Despite herself, she smiled. "Where do you think?"

His eyes lit up with amusement. "That's a dangerous game."

"Are you afraid to play?" The words surprised her once she'd spoken them. It was unlike her to be so playful with a stranger. She was normally cautious, reserved. A cat of a person.

He dropped her hand, and she felt a panicked thud inside her chest. Here in the fading outside afternoon light, she was able to get a better look at his face. He was handsome for sure, but he was not by any means the best-looking man she'd ever seen. His skin showed damage from teenage acne and his nose hooked slightly to the right, but there was something about him. A magnetism. A fire. A charm that made him more handsome than he should've been.

"No," he said. "Should I be?"

"Very," she said.

And just then, she realized that she had been wrong before. His blue eyes didn't remind her of home. Nothing about him felt like home.

He reminded her of America. Of her American dream.

VII.

"We're here," Julian said.

"You can't stop there," Harlow said, and I felt the same way, though I was in too much of a daze to really say anything. Imagining my mother at that age—only a few years older than me now—required as much of a suspension of disbelief as envisioning dragons. It was nearly impossible to picture her as anything other than the polished, put-together older person I knew her to be. "Seriously," Harlow pushed. "It was just starting to get good. You apparently had some game."

I squirmed at this comment, and Julian laughed lightly. Wearily. "Don't worry, girls. I promise I'll tell you more later." He glanced at me. "But now it's time to meet your grandma, Tal."

We pulled up in front of a white farmhouse. It sat on the top of a gentle hill, and a large oak dominated the left side of the yard. It was surrounded by acres and acres of rolling grass. In the darkness, I couldn't make out many details, but there was a low glow coming from the porch light that illuminated four well-worn rocking chairs.

Home, my mind instantly thought. And then, *No*, it quickly corrected.

It's funny how some places just feel familiar in your bones, even if you've never been there before. I studied the rocking chairs—solid wood, solid craftsmanship—and wondered if Mom had ever been here. If she'd ever sat on that porch, legs up, chatting happily with Julian as the sun sank lower and lower into the sky. I wondered if Julian would tell Harlow and me about that later.

Thinking about that scene made something inside me ache in both a good and a bad way.

I was about to ask if we were just going to sit in the car all night when the front door of the white farmhouse flung open. A squat woman stepped out onto the porch. She was wrapped in a cream-colored terry-cloth robe and her sheet-white hair was piled high on her head.

"JP?" she called out. Her voice had a noticeable Southern drawl to it. "Is that you?"

"JP?" Harlow said. "Who the hell is JP?"

"Julian Parker Oliver," I answered before he could say anything.

"Right," he said softly. "That's what my family calls me."

"Oh," said Harlow.

Julian took a deep breath. "All right. Here we go." He stepped out of the car, and Harlow and I followed suit.

"Mama," he called out as he walked toward the porch. Harlow and I followed behind him.

"You made it," she said, and I detected something in her voice. Surprise? Bitterness, maybe. Or at least the hollow ring of sadness.

"Mama," he repeated. "I told you I would come. And I'm here."

Something like relief washed over her face. Her eyes lit up as she pulled Julian into a long embrace. As Harlow and I got closer, I could see that her eyes were the same glacier blue as mine.

"Oh my," she breathed as we got closer. "Who are these girls, JP?" She grimaced. "They are much too young for you. Are you ladies even eighteen?"

Her eyes narrowed as she studied me. And then she gasped. "Oh my heavens." She clasped her hand over her heart and turned to Julian. "JP, is she . . . ?"

He nodded. "Lena's."

Her gaze flitted from Julian to me and back again. "Those eyes, though . . ."

He nodded again. "Meet Taliah. Your granddaughter."

She gasped again and clutched at the neckline of her robe. "Granddaughter?" She turned to Julian for clarification.

"It's a long story," he said in a slow and stilted way.

"A long story, huh?" she pushed.

"Mama, I promise to tell you everything, but it's late." I could hear the desperation in his voice; it made me feel unbearably awkward.

Her eyes flitted from Julian to me and back again. "I don't know what to say. . . ."

I stared down at my sneakers, debating whether or not I should walk back to the car. "I'm sorry," I finally managed to say.

"Sorry?" she exclaimed. "Sweetheart, you have nothing to be sorry for." She walked toward me and clutched my face in her hands. "I'm so glad your father has finally brought you home."

Home, my brain repeated. *H-O-M-E*. So many mysteries, so many feelings, so many questions wrapped up in those four letters.

DAY TWO

(In Which I Learn About the Multiplicity of Self)

I.

I woke up before Harlow. It took me a moment or two to remember where I was. The creaky twin mattress and plaid comforter were startlingly unfamiliar. I rolled over onto my side and groaned, and then groggily slipped out of bed. I pulled my jeans back on. I'd slept in my striped T-shirt from yesterday. I sniffed it. It had at least another day left in it.

I crept down the hallway. The other bedroom doors were still closed tight. I checked my phone and saw it was only 6:03 a.m. I never woke up that early, but I guess my body knew I was in a different and strange place, so it decided to adjust accordingly by doing different and strange things.

I had bad reception in Oak Falls, but after a few painful seconds my phone dinged and I saw an email from Mom pop up. Harlow always compares my relationship with my Mom to Lorelai and Rory Gilmore's, but I take some issue with that comparison. First, I feel like any mom and daughter who are close and the mom is relatively attractive get compared to Lorelai and Rory.

Admittedly Mom and I are pretty inseparable, which is basically the only way to be when it's just the two of us. We have our routines—sushi night on Tuesdays at Hiro, and Saturday-afternoon movie matinees at the Edgecliff. I'm almost always her date to any of her academic functions or gallery openings, and we help each other get dressed, offering advice (that is sometimes taken, sometimes not) on shoes and lipstick color.

But Mom is much stricter than Lorelai. Or maybe I just feel that way because I'm her daughter.

I touched the screen to open the email. I held my breath, feeling impossibly guilty. I hadn't even technically lied to her yet, and still. The withholding of information almost felt worse. Especially when I was used to sharing almost everything with Mom.

HB,

Good morning from Paris! I walked the streets around my hotel this morning and treated myself to a pain au chocolat and a café au lait, which made me miss you so much as I remembered our last trip here and how I think you ate the whole country of France out of pain au chocolat!

I'm heading over to the gallery this afternoon to preview the space. I'm feeling very excited about the talent they've booked for the opening. Should be wonderful. I might bop over to the Cluny afterwards. Do you remember how much you loved the unicorn tapestries? Exquisite.

How are you? Is Harlow still there? I hope you girls are behaving and not getting yourself into too much trouble. Remember you can always call my cell phone if there's an emergency, but no need to pay the long-distance charges if everything is fine.

Have I already told you I miss you? I miss you, my sweet girl.

Xo,

Mom

Mom always addresses me as **HB** in our correspondence. It's an inside joke of sorts. She calls me *habibti*, the blanket

Arabic endearment. And since she claims "kids these days" abbreviate everything, she started calling me "HB" and it stuck.

I fiddled with my phone, my fingers anxiously hovering over the screen. I finally decided on a quick but simple reply:

> Hi! Sounds like you are having lots of fun! Harlow and I are fine. We're also having an interesting time. Will tell you about it when you get home!
>
> Love you,
>
> Tal

Not a lie, but not exactly the truth. I wish there was a word for that middle ground. It should be "truelie" or something like that.

I put my phone back in my pocket and continued to creep down the hall. When I reached the study, I saw the door was halfway open. I peeked inside and spotted Julian passed out on his side on the futon. He hadn't even bothered to put sheets on it. I debated waking him up, but decided against it.

I padded down the wooden staircase that was covered with a shaggy oatmeal-colored carpet runner. The kitchen was empty. Last night when Grandma—or Debra, as I was still referring to her because it was too much to just call her Grandma (or rather, Nana, as she'd requested) right off the bat—invited us in, she'd pulled several casseroles out of the refrigerator and heated them.

"Folks don't know what to do about the fact that Tom's . . ." she'd said, trailing off as she unwrapped the tinfoil off of one of the casseroles. The reality of Tom's state hovered silently in the air. She squeezed her eyes shut for a second and let out an audible exhale. She turned to face me. "The people around here are very kind. What they lack in knowledge of what to say, they make up for in casserole-making. God bless the people of Oak Falls."

Once Debra had heated all the casseroles, she gave me a pointed look. "You're my first granddaughter. It's been all boys until you. And I want to know every single thing about you, but tomorrow we're going to the hospital to possibly say good-bye to my husband of fifty-two years. And so for the time being, I need to be in my room." She paused and her eyes drifted from me to Julian. "I fixed up the upstairs guest room with the hope that you'd come home, JP. But now that you're all here, why don't you take the futon in . . ." She paused again and a pained look came over her face. She pursed her lips together and shook her head like she was fighting against the tornado of emotions brewing inside of her.

"Mama, it's okay," Julian said softly. "I'll make sure the girls get set up in the guest room, and don't you worry about me. I'll find somewhere to sleep."

She nodded and gave him a look like she was seeing a

ghost. "I'll see you all in the morning" was all she said, and then she left the kitchen.

We all took halfhearted bites of meaty lasagna and cheesy broccoli and Harlow and Julian helped themselves to second servings of a potato bake that was sprinkled with bacon. (Perhaps the only Islamic tradition observed in our household was that Mom and I didn't eat any pork products, and I couldn't bring myself to eat the bacon. I already felt guilty enough as it was.)

"You don't want any?" Julian asked, pushing the potato bake dish closer to me.

I shook my head. "I don't eat bacon."

Julian paused and set his fork down on the table. He gave me a curious look. "But I thought you said you weren't religious."

I shrugged. I was too overwhelmed to try to explain the detailed nuances of the rules my mother had set.

"Well, I think I'm going to follow Mom's lead and go to bed, too," Julian said. "I'm an old man these days and today has been . . . long."

"It's only eleven," Harlow protested. "You should take us somewhere cool in Oak Falls."

I kicked Harlow under the table. I wanted her to knock it off. I was also tired, and lying down sounded really good to me, even if I wasn't certain I would be able to get to sleep.

"It's Oak Falls," Julian deadpanned. "There's nothing cool."

"Come on," Harlow said. "You're Julian Oliver. You must know of something cool. Isn't Oak Falls a college town?"

"JP," I said without thinking.

He gave me a weak smile. "Yes. In this house, I'm JP. Not Julian Oliver."

"And JP is your lame alter ego?" Harlow teased.

He shrugged and a long silence stretched between us. I kept waiting for him to get up and go to bed like he'd declared he was going to, but instead he stayed planted at the breakfast bar, dragging his fork through the meaty lasagna.

"JP is my best self," Julian finally said, sounding like one of those new age-y self-help books.

"Your best self?" I asked tentatively.

"Yes," he said. "It just took me a long time to realize it." His eyes went hazy and I assumed he was thinking about his dad. Or maybe Mom. "Maybe, really, it actually took me until now to."

As much as I wanted to push him to elaborate on that, I couldn't. I didn't know how to enter such a personal space with him. It had always been just Mom and me. I knew how to talk to Mom about anything. Well, anything other than Julian.

A nervousness nibbled in my stomach and I stood up from my chair. "Well, I'm going to go to bed, too."

"Taliah?" Julian said.

"Yes?"

"Are you okay?"

"I don't know," I said, because it was the most honest answer.

"Me either."

I stood frozen in the kitchen for a brief moment. So far, being in the Oliver household had been like living inside a movie that was playing at half speed. Each action was elongated; too much time was allotted to overanalyze and agonize over the meaning of every single gesture, every quip. I needed someone to press fast-forward.

But maybe half speed was the side effect of grief. I wasn't familiar enough with loss or the anticipation of it to really know.

I gave Julian a halfhearted wave and glanced at Harlow, who was absorbed in her phone. "See you guys in the morning."

And now it was morning. I slipped outside the front door, and even though it was early, the sun was already high in the sky. It fell against my skin as I ambled along the edge of the property, ducking under the shade of some tall and leafy oak trees that were planted beside the white equestrian-style fence that snaked around the Olivers' land.

The property seemed to stretch on endlessly. As far as I could see, there were grassy, rolling hills. An earthy musk floated in the air. It smelled like mud. And maybe cows. I squinted, trying to catch sight of any livestock, but I couldn't spot any. I craned my neck to look over at the other side of the fence.

"Hey," an unfamiliar voice called out.

I froze, unsure whether I should turn around.

"Hello?" the voice called again.

I stayed in the shade of the oaks and started to run back toward the farmhouse. I kept my eyes down out of fear of making accidental eye contact and focused on the grass, which was wet with morning dew and tickled my ankles.

Even with my face aimed down, I could see the house emerging on the horizon. I let out a deep breath of relief and then I felt my body collide against someone else. I tumbled backwards with a thud, and splayed out in the damp grass.

"Oh dang!" the same voice from before howled. "You okay?"

A hand stretched out in my direction. I didn't have the courage to glance up at the face that went along with the hand.

The hand didn't move. "You came home with JP, right?"

I refused to grasp the outstretched hand and instead helped myself up. Once I was back on my own two feet, I took a deep breath. The face I found in front of me was warm. It belonged to a guy who appeared to be about my age. He was sun-freckled, with floppy auburn hair that curled up around his ears. It was long in a way that seemed hip, but the length somehow seemed less like a purposeful style choice and more related to a lack of attention. He was wearing a gray baseball cap. He had wide brown eyes that reminded me of a puppy in the best sort of way. My body, at odds with my anxious mind, slowly relaxed.

"Yes," I said, my eyes flitting around his face, unsure where to settle. "I'm Julian's daughter," I said without thinking, and then instantly regretted it.

"I know," he said. "Word travels fast around here."

"I've been here less than twelve hours."

"Your cousins told me," he explained.

"My cousins?"

"Yeah. Brady and Carter."

I tried not to look as clueless as I felt. "Brady and Carter," I repeated.

He gave me a self-assured grin that I probably would've found charming a few moments ago, but now found irritating. "Yeah. I know you don't know who they are. But they know who you are."

I forced myself to laugh. "That's a little creepy."

"There's not much happening here in Oak Falls. Especially on this side of town. And especially amongst us townies." He gestured toward the other side of the fence. "I live next door. I'm Toby, by the way." He stuck his hand back out again.

I tentatively shook it. Treating it as though it were a hot potato. A quick grab, shake, and drop.

"I'm Taliah."

"Yeah. I know," he said, the self-assured grin reappearing on his face. I didn't know anyone who was that happy. If anything, the people I knew often pretended to be less happy than they were.

"I'm sorry about Tom," he offered.

"I've never met him," I said in a way that I'd hoped would sound frank and actually came out sounding a little callous. I winced.

"Then I'm sorry about that." Toby looked like he was about to say something else, but instead played with the bill of his baseball cap. "So what are you doing up so early?"

"I'm a morning person."

He squinted at me. "I'm going to call bunk on that."

"Bunk?"

He shrugged, and I saw a bit of self-consciousness cross his face. "Hooey. You know . . ."

"Bullshit," I filled in. "And you are right. But how'd you know?"

He shrugged again. "I'm a good guesser."

"Right," I said, and then added, as if I had to explain my early-morning activities to Toby, "I don't sleep well in strange places."

"Understandable," he said, and despite my aversion to

it before, I made eye contact with him. He was admittedly very cute, though I felt like that was probably one of the last things he would want you to notice about him, which somehow made him cuter. Goddamnit.

"What?" he said after I'd stared him down for a good minute.

"I'm just trying to figure you out."

He laughed. "And you think you can figure out us simple folks from Oak Falls just by staring at us for a moment or two?"

I blanched. "No, no. That's not it at all."

"Then what is it?"

"I don't know. You're being incredibly friendly to someone you don't know."

Toby whistled to himself.

"What?" I asked, feeling a little self-conscious.

"I just find it very interesting that you're characterizing my behavior as 'very friendly.' Maybe Brady and Carter were right about you."

"Excuse me?" It took me a second to process that my cousins, who, up until a few moments ago, I hadn't even known existed, had already judged me. These were the moments when I was convinced Mom was right about the human race—the majority of people should not be trusted.

"They figured you'd be . . ." He looked nervous. Some of his bravado had faded.

"I'd be?" I prompted.

"You know. Think you're better than all of us since you're Julian Oliver's daughter."

Before I had a chance to say anything, Toby continued, "But I thought they might be judging you too quickly. So I figured I'd check you out for myself."

"Right," I said dryly. "And what's your assessment?"

"Jury's still out," he said pleasantly, and fiddled with the bill of his baseball cap again. He leaned his back against the fence.

"Did you just hop over that when you saw me walking around?"

He nodded proudly. "Guilty as charged."

"Is that allowed? Hopping onto someone else's property like that?"

"Depends who's asking. You'd be surprised. The crazy stuff that goes down here in Oak Falls."

I laughed. "Okay then." I briefly relished the fact that Toby had the distinct privilege of being the first boy to hop over a fence to talk to me. And then felt embarrassed by the fact I was relishing that at all.

Your grandfather is dying, I reminded myself.

But you don't even know him, my mind argued.

But still, my conscience fired back.

"Let's walk down to the lake," he said, as if that was the most natural suggestion in the whole world.

"The lake?"

Toby pointed off into the distance. "Yeah. There's a lake that sits at the far edge of your property." Then he quickly corrected himself. "Of your grandparents' property." And then corrected himself again. "Of Debra's property."

"And this lake is one of the things that will reveal Oak Falls to have more going on than meets the eye?"

He glanced at me, an unreadable expression on his face. It began to dawn on me that Toby was the word "earnest" in living form. I could easily imagine him dressed in an Eagle Scout uniform, passing out canned goods to homeless people on a snowy Christmas Eve. I began to wonder if I'd crossed some imaginary line. Like it was okay for him to joke about Oak Falls being small and boring and provincial, but not okay for me to do so.

"I dunno," he said slowly. "I figured you might just want to see it since it's one of your grandfather's favorite places."

"Really?" Something inside me thrummed with a curiosity I hadn't known I had.

"Yeah. When I was younger, he used to take me, Brady, and Carter down there to fish." Toby let out a laugh that wasn't really a laugh but more the mere echo of one. "I really liked your grandfather. He was a special guy." And then he quickly corrected himself. "I mean like. And is. Present tense."

He flashed me an apologetic look and I shrugged. "The

verbiage is difficult, huh?" I said.

He nodded somberly. "I love Tom. You see, I lost my dad when I was six, so Tom tried to be like, I don't know, a father figure of sorts. When I was younger, he used to invite me over on Saturday afternoons and we'd build model airplanes together with your cousins. He really welcomed me into your family."

It felt impossibly weird to hear them described as my family when I wouldn't have been able to pick Tom or my cousins out of a lineup.

"He sounds like a nice guy," I offered. "But I wouldn't really know."

Toby nodded thoughtfully. "You and Julian didn't want to hang out here too much, huh?"

I stopped walking and gaped at Toby. "What are you talking about? I didn't even really know for sure that Julian was my father until yesterday afternoon."

He turned to face me. He took off his baseball cap and passed it back and forth between his hands. "I had no clue. I just assumed you lived in New York City or somewhere fancy with Julian."

I fought back a laugh. "Trust me, I'm not from New York. I live about five hours away in a place just as boring as this one."

"Hey," Toby said, his grin back. "Oak Falls isn't boring. I'm going to prove that to you."

Toby started walking again, his pace quickening like we needed to make good time. The air was getting stickier by the moment and the sun was climbing higher and higher in the sky. Also, the cow scent had not dissipated.

"I mean, there obviously was something wrong between Julian and Tom, right?" I asked. I was fishing, I knew, but I couldn't help it.

"I dunno," Toby said slowly. "I just know Julian didn't come home a lot."

"Well, I think he's pretty busy, you know?" I was surprised by the defensive tone in my voice.

"Yeah," Toby said quietly. "We all get it. He's a big rock star, but I don't think that gives you a free pass to be a jerk to your family."

"He's been a jerk to his family?"

"Look, it's not really my place to talk about this," Toby said tentatively. "You should probably ask Julian."

"Okay," I said. "Well, I just want to clear the air."

Toby glanced at me, his eyes widened as if bracing for me to say something of marked import.

"Something smells like cows. And it's not me."

His shoulders hunched forward and he laughed. This time it was not a mere echo, but the real deal. And it was lovely. We were about to head down another hill when I heard Harlow bellowing, "Taliah Abdallat!"

"Uh," I said, audibly swallowing. "That's my friend."

Toby nodded. He looked amused.

Within a few minutes, Harlow had caught up to us. Her face was flushed red from running and she was panting. Her hair was pulled into a messy low ponytail. She looked from Toby to me and back again, and then cast me a teasing smile. I gave her the don't-you-dare glare and she laughed.

"You ran off."

"I, unlike you, didn't run anywhere."

Her teasing smile widened. "Okay, smartass. Everyone is looking for you." She turned again to Toby. "I'm Harlow, by the way. No one understands why I'm here, but I am."

I nudged my shoulder against Harlow's. "She's here because she's my best friend."

Toby stuck out his hand. "I'm Toby. I live next door."

Harlow shook his hand. "Hello, Toby who lives next door. It's nice to meet you. But if you'll forgive me, I need to steal our girl back. People are looking for her."

Toby's brown eyes met mine. "All righty then." He shoved his hands into the pockets of his jeans. "Maybe we can check out that lake some other time, huh?"

"Yeahsureokay," I mumbled.

Harlow locked her arm with mine and we spun around and started walking back toward the Oliver farmhouse when I heard Toby call out, "Taliah?"

I turned back around. "Yeah?"

"It's good that you're here."

I squinted at him in the sunlight. "I hope so."

Harlow tugged at my arm. "We really have to go."

I gave Toby a little wave and then started back toward the farmhouse. When we were a good distance from him, Harlow started needling me. "He's cute."

"Who?" I said, playing dumb.

"You know, if I were into that," Harlow added, elbowing me.

"Right."

"How'd you meet him?"

"Oh. You know. The way you meet people in Oak Falls," I deadpanned. "Hopping fences."

"Cute." And then she repeated, "He's cute."

"He's my grandmother-who-I-don't-know-at-all's neighbor. He's grieving my grandfather-who-I-never-knew-at-all. They're apparently close. And he's also apparently friends with my cousins who I've never met but already hate me."

Harlow swatted at a mosquito.

"So?"

"Aren't you concerned at all that my cousins already hate me?"

Harlow shrugged. "They'll come around. I'm more focused on cute boy for now."

"He lives in Oak Falls."

"So? You're always full of excuses, Tal."

"Harlow. My grandfather is dying."

"Yeah," she said softly. "I know. But still. The boy's cute."

We were close to the back porch. I saw Julian sitting alone in a wooden rocker. "This doesn't exactly seem like the right time for romance, you know? There's already too many new people in my life."

Harlow didn't say anything to that. She just squeezed my arm.

II.

"You don't have to be nervous," Julian said, glancing at me in the rearview mirror. Harlow and I were once again seated in the back of his Mustang. We were headed to the hospital to see Tom. Though I couldn't stop wondering if we were really headed to see Tom or just the final shadow of him.

The thought made me shudder.

"Right," I said. "You keep saying that. But it seems like you're the one who's nervous."

He fiddled with his sunglasses, pushing them up on the

bridge of his nose. "You're probably right."

I swallowed. "When's the last time you saw him?"

Julian let out a long, audible sigh and winced a little. "Eh. I think five years ago. Christmas? Maybe."

"Five years ago?"

He shrugged. Harlow glanced down at her phone. I think she could sense the conversation was about to take an awkwardly personal turn and she wanted to be as inconspicuous as possible.

"Dad and I don't . . ." He trailed off and took a sharp right turn. I jerked with the movement of the car, my shoulder bumping against Harlow's. "We don't," he continued, "have the best relationship."

I opened my mouth to ask why, but he cut me off.

"I disappointed him," he said plainly. "Though I probably shouldn't put that as past tense. As long as he's still breathing, I'm disappointing him."

"That's a pretty intense thing to say," I said slowly.

"Yeah," he agreed. "But sadly that doesn't make it any less true."

"What went wrong?" Harlow asked bluntly, and then gave me an apologetic smile.

"Shit," Julian mused, fiddling with his sunglasses again. "What didn't go wrong?"

"That's not an answer," I pointed out.

"Okay," Julian said, barking out a hollow laugh. "Well, here it is, cold and simple and straight up: I followed my dream at the cost of ruining my dad's."

He continued, "My dad owned a small homemade furniture store near campus. His dad had owned it before him. The stuff they sold there was simple—stools, rockers. My grandfather made the furniture by hand from the wood he got from chopping down trees on his land. He passed the trade down to Dad, along with the land. And so Dad, of course, had high hopes and big dreams that I'd continue the legacy."

Julian paused. We were stopped at a red light. He let out a heavy breath. "But do you know what I find more interesting than woodworking?"

"Music?" I asked softly.

"Yeah. That. And everything else." Another hollow laugh. "Your mom and I had that in common, you know? It was one of the first things we connected over."

I wrinkled my nose. "A disinterest in woodworking?"

"Well, no. But the shared fear of disappointing our parents. Because their dreams for us were diametrically opposed with our dreams for ourselves."

Harlow perked back up. "Tell us more." And then clarified, "About you and Lena."

Julian rubbed his right temple. "Mm. Okay. Where did I leave off?"

"The diner," I said, an eagerness creeping into my voice.

"The diner," he said, making eye contact with me through the rearview mirror. "Right."

L ena made a face as she bit into her hamburger.

Julian looked crestfallen. "You don't like it?"

"The meat," she said, chewing slowly and slightly embarrassed to be talking while eating, "isn't . . . cooked?" She put her burger back down on the plate. She took her knife and cut into the meat to show him the revolting pink splotches.

He laughed. "That's a perfectly cooked burger. You don't want it too well done. The meat would be burned all to hell." He took a long slurp of his vanilla milk shake.

She wrinkled her nose.

"You eat burnt burgers where you're from?"

She smiled slightly. *Where you're from.* "At twenty-one May Street? Yes."

He nodded, matching her smile and following along with her joke. "Yes. I've heard that May Street has a reputation for only permitting overcooked burgers." He popped a fry into his mouth. "But seriously. Are you going to tell me where you're from?"

She considered continuing to be wry, but decided against it. "Jordan. Do you know where that is?"

"Vaguely," he said, and then quickly confessed, "Not really."

"In the Middle East. Sandwiched between Israel, Syria, Iraq, and Saudi Arabia." An idea popped into her head. "Do you have a pen?"

Julian smiled and produced one. "I do, in fact. My server's pen. For all the orders I'm currently not taking."

She drew a sloppy map of the Middle East on her napkin. She showed it to him. "There's Jordan."

He propped his elbows up on the table. "Do you miss it?"

"Yes." She smiled again. "Especially the burnt meat."

"What brought you here?"

She was about to use her standard response about studying medicine. The one she'd rehearsed for years. The one she'd almost convinced herself of. But instead she said, "I came to be an artist."

His face lit up. "An artist? What type of art?"

She shrugged and nibbled at one of her fries. "I haven't decided yet. Technically, I'm studying biology at Hampton."

"Biology?" He rolled the word over his tongue. "That's an odd choice for a budding artist."

"My mother thinks I came to America to become a doctor," she explained.

"Ah. I understand that."

"You do?"

"My parents think I'm working at the diner to save money to be able to go to college."

"And you aren't?"

He grinned and shook his head. "Well, most of the time, I'm not even working. And when I am, I'm saving money to move to New York. You see, my father owns a store." Something crossed over his face. "The store, it's close to here, actually. And he wants me to take it over. It was his dad's before it was his, so it's kind of this family thing."

Lena nodded along. "But you don't want to run the store?"

Julian shook his head again. "No. And I don't want to make wooden stools for the rest of my life. But to get my dad off my back, I told him that I was going to go to college so that I could be more book smart when it came to running the store. Business degree or some shit."

"But that's not your plan?"

"Naw," he said, his grin back, stretching wider this time. "I'm going to be a musician."

"A musician?"

"Yeah." He locked his eyes with hers. "I want to write songs that make people feel new things. And remember things they've forgotten." He paused and tapped his knuckles against the table. "I want to write your favorite song."

Lena blushed. His sheer confidence in his dream was infectious. It made her want to believe more deeply in her own.

When she didn't say anything, he added, "Isn't it perfect?"

"What?"

"This."

She smirked. "I already told you the burger wasn't cooked properly."

"No, silly," he said, and the word "silly" very much felt like its meaning as it slipped from his mouth. "This. Us meeting. Someday we're both going to be killing it in New York. You a badass artist. Me a badass musician."

She considered this, tilting her head to the side. "I don't know how I feel about New York."

"But what if I'm in New York?"

"Aren't you getting ahead of yourself?"

"Always," he said with a grin. And then something crossed his face. "I'm Julian, by the way." He stretched his hand across the table in a way that seemed overly formal considering the bizarre intimateness of their encounter so far.

When she would replay this afternoon over again in her head, as she would do multiple times over the years to come, she always found it strange how time didn't seem to exist in her memory. The afternoon felt both like an eternity and a fleeting blip. Maybe all of life's most defining moments were like that.

She shook his hand. "Lena."

"Lena. I should've known you would have a perfect name."

"What makes a perfect name?"

"One that perfectly suits the face it is assigned to."

She studied his face. The faded acne scars. The hooked nose. The piercing, expressive eyes. "I don't think Julian is the perfect name for you, then."

This seemed to amuse him. "Oh, really?" He raised his eyebrows dramatically. "Then tell me, Lena, what would be a better name for me?"

She shrugged and dragged a fry through a dollop of ketchup. She was still in the process of determining whether or not she liked the condiment. Most days, she found it to be too sweet. But in this particular moment, she didn't mind it so much. "What's your last name?"

"Oliver."

"Okay." She popped the fry into her mouth, the burst of salt and sweet tomato paste tangoing on her tongue. "I think that's better. I'm going to call you Oliver."

"You, Lena," he said in a theatrical voice, "can call me anything."

She smiled wide despite herself. Wide smiles revealed the noticeable gap in her bottom teeth and enhanced her dimples. "Aren't you getting ahead of yourself again?"

His eyes shone. "Always."

III.

"What the hell, Oliver!" Harlow said as we pulled into the parking lot of Oak Falls Memorial Hospital. "You're a sadist. You can't leave us hanging like that."

I had to agree with Harlow. I wanted *more, more, more.* But even as Julian filled in certain blanks for me—how my mom met him, when she met him—more blanks appeared. Wider and more nagging. *When did it go wrong? How did it go wrong?*

I wanted to know. And I also didn't.

Unlike Harlow, I'd never liked sad stories.

"Sorry, lady," Julian said to Harlow, but he was looking at me. "Got to stop for now. We're here."

I moved to get out of the car, but Harlow stayed planted in her seat. "Tal," she said.

"Yeah?"

"Is it okay with you if I just wait on a bench outside the hospital?"

I nodded. Julian stepped out of the car, presumably to let me and Harlow talk in private.

"I want to be there for you," she said.

"I know."

"But it feels weird."

"It feels weird to me, too."

She gave me a knowing look and then stared down at her chipped nail polish. "I know. But it's different. You . . ."

"I . . . ?"

"You should be here," she finally said. "This is your family."

"But I don't know them," I said, and then amended, "Well, I barely know them."

"That's the point, though, right? That's why you should be here. To get to know them."

Out of the corner of my eye, I caught sight of Julian watching us.

"You should go," Harlow said firmly. "I'll be right here." She paused and then looked out the window and gestured. "Or right there." She pulled volume three of *Saga* out of her

112

oversized canvas tote bag. "I even brought reading materials."

She reached over to hug me. "I feel like I should say good
luck, but that doesn't sound right. So I'll just say I love you,
okay?"

"I love you too," I said, and stepped out of the car. It felt
good to say that aloud and to hear her say it too. When we
were younger, we used to tell each other "I love you" all the
time, but as we got older, we stopped saying it. Like it was
stupid to repeat something we already knew. But sometimes
you need to say things aloud. It makes them feel real. And
after the few weird months that Harlow and I'd had, I was
glad it was starting to feel real again.

As Julian and I walked toward the front entrance to the
hospital, he asked, "Is everything okay?"

"Yeah," I said, staring down at the cement sidewalk. "I
mean, I don't know. I guess?"

He laughed a little and slung his arm around my shoulder. His touch startled me. It was still weird. One part of
my mind understood this was my father. But the other part
still had difficulty separating that from the fact that this was
a man who had been on the cover of *Rolling Stone*. "I know
what you mean."

I wasn't sure that he did, but maybe. It felt like thousands
of question marks were floating in the air, and instead of

grabbing them out of the air and shaking them for answers, we were simply accepting the mystery of the moment.

The automated front doors slid open and a rush of cool air greeted us. Julian steered us toward the elevator bank. As we waited to go up, he said, "I don't want it to be like this for us."

Something inside me turned. I felt a swell of emotion—it reminded me of how I felt the first time I listened to one of Julian's songs—an overwhelming feeling of sadness and uncertainty, but somehow there was also a trace of hope. I untucked myself from under his arm so I could look up at his face.

When I didn't say anything, he continued, "I don't want to wait until I'm dying to make things right between us."

The elevator doors dinged open and we stepped inside. It was only us in the small box headed up to the fourth floor.

"I regret that a lot, you know?" he said. His face was solemn, but his eyes were hazy. "That I waited this long to see my dad. And now I won't ever have the chance to make amends with him."

We stepped out of the elevator. I started to walk down the hallway, but he put his hand on my shoulder and stopped me.

"Taliah," he said, looking me straight in the eye. "When someone's dying, we make it all about the firsts and the lasts. We recount things from the beginning and from the end, but we hardly ever talk about the middle. But it's the middle that matters, you know?"

I nodded, even though I wasn't quite sure. "I know I missed your beginning, but what I'm trying to say is, I don't want to miss the middle. I want to be there for the meat of your life. I don't want to just show up at the end in a hurried attempt to put a bow on all my mistakes."

I broke away from his gaze. "I get that," I said slowly.

"You do?" he pressed.

"I do. But I also think that this moment isn't really about you and me. It's about you and your dad." I shuffled my feet.

"It's about us, too," he urged. He looked like he was about to say something else, but then I followed his gaze to Debra and another woman who were standing outside the doorway of one of the hospital rooms.

"There's Mom," Julian said. "And my sister, Sarah."

Sarah looked like a younger version of Debra. She had the same squat build, but her hair hadn't whitened. It was a cornmeal blond, only slightly darker than Julian's. And she, like all the Olivers I'd met so far, had the same glacier eyes. My eyes.

They walked toward us. Sarah and Debra were even dressed alike. In flowing, loose-fitting, flower-patterned smock dresses. Sarah, though, had a few more "granola" touches to her ensemble—Birkenstocks and a bag made of recycled materials that advertised a clean water charity. I'd later learn that Sarah worked as a third-grade teacher at the local elementary school.

"Julian," Sarah said. It wasn't exactly warm. But it wasn't cold either. "You're here."

"Of course I'm here, Sarah."

Sarah's eyes fell on me. "And you must be Taliah."

I gave a little wave. "Nice to meet you."

"I loved your mother," she said. Her voice cracked a bit, and she raised her hand to her mouth as if she wanted to swallow her sadness back. "I'm sorry," she said quickly, not looking at Julian or me in particular. "It's just a hard day."

"You don't have to apologize," I said gently. *I loved your mother.* That sentence didn't have to be past tense. Mom was still alive. Mom was in Paris. Clueless about all of this.

She looked at me again. "Can I hug you?"

Before I had a chance to respond, she had enveloped me in a warm and sweaty hug. I had thought her hug was going to make me feel uncomfortable, but there was something comforting about it. Something unexpectedly familiar. When she finally pulled away, she dabbed at her eyes.

"This is all . . . it's all, just, a lot, you know?" she said to Julian.

He nodded in agreement. "I know it is. Where are the bear cubs?"

I slowly caught on that the bear cubs to whom he was

referring were Sarah's two boys, Brady and Carter—my two cousins who had apparently already been gossiping about me to Toby. It felt weird to know I'd been the subject of speculation. And even weirder to know that all of that speculation was driven by the fact that I was linked to Julian.

Sarah explained to Julian that the boys were at home with their father, Todd. "You know, JP," she said, "they aren't really bear cubs anymore. They're twelve." She glanced at me and offered, "Twins."

I shuffled my feet uncomfortably.

"And you're . . . ?" Sarah asked.

"Sixteen," I answered.

"So a little bit older. I've been trying to figure out how to handle this with them. You know, whenever situations like this come up with one of my students, I always advise parents to handle things head-on. And the boys are obviously much older than my students now. But I've still been shielding them from this." She shook her head and stared at the ground. "I just don't know."

"I'm sure you'll figure it out, Sar," Julian said generously. "You're a fantastic mother."

"How would you know?" Sarah said, and the sharpness in her voice startled me. It was such a change from the melancholy wistfulness of before. "You haven't been around at all to see how I am as a mother. My boys wouldn't know who you are if it weren't for MTV."

"MTV." Julian shook his head. "There's no music on MTV anymore. I'm definitely not on MTV frequently. At least I don't think I am." He turned to me, a jokey glint in his eye. "Am I on MTV?"

I shrugged. I wasn't about to get in the middle of whatever was brewing between them.

"That's not the point," Sarah snapped. "You know what I mean."

"Yeah, I know," Julian said.

Sarah tugged on her tote bag's strap. "Do you, though? Do you, JP?"

"I'm here now," Julian said firmly.

"And what? You want a trophy for that?"

"Sarah," Debra finally interjected. She clasped her hands together. "Now is not the time to fight."

"So what? We're just supposed to pretend like everything's okay?"

Debra's lips moved like she was about to say something, but Julian cut her off. "Look, I know I've made a lot of mistakes. And I haven't been home as much as I should've been, but railing into me isn't going to make Dad better."

Sarah hung her head.

"How is he?" Julian asked, and I watched him glance at the door to his father's hospital room.

"Still unconscious," Debra said. "The doctors . . ."

Debra sniffled and Sarah put her hand on her shoulder. She continued for Debra, "The doctors say the stroke was severe. His heart is giving out and his brain activity is slowing." Her voice cracked. "We're losing him, Julian. This is it."

Julian's face went blank. Stoic. He shoved his hands into the pockets of his skinny jeans. He let out an audible breath. "I'm gonna go see him, okay?" he said, half asking.

Sarah and Debra nodded.

"I want you to meet him," Julian said to me. He looked desperate and frantic. He kept tapping his left foot. "But I've got to say a few things to him first, all right?"

As Julian walked into the hospital room, Debra steered me and Sarah toward a bench in the hallway. Once we were all sitting down, Debra folded her hands and placed them on her lap. She sighed heavily.

"The doctors say it's going to be up to us to decide. But how do you decide something like that?" Debra pulled a Kleenex out of her bag and dabbed her eyes.

Sarah put her hands on top of her mother's. "Mom. Don't you worry about that right now."

"Sarah, sweet pea," Debra said, her voice soothing like a lullaby. "That's the only thing I can worry about right now. We're gonna have to make that choice, you know? Us. There's no one else to do it."

"I know," Sarah said, resigned.

A few tears trickled down Debra's cheeks. They pooled into her wrinkles. "How, though? How will we know when it's time?"

My throat ached. I wanted to cry, but I wasn't able to. And I wasn't sure why. Probably because it didn't feel like this grief—their grief—was mine. That I deserved to share in it.

I was sad. But I was sad for all the wrong reasons.

Sad that I'd never get to meet my grandfather. At least not when he was conscious and present.

Sad that all of them, including my own father, were strangers to me.

"Do you guys want some privacy?" I asked. I stared at the room Julian had entered, wishing he'd come out, but also nervous for him to do so because then I'd have to go in.

Sarah and Debra shook their heads. "No. You're a part of this family too."

"I know, but—"

Debra cut me off by squeezing my shoulder. "No buts about it, my dear."

"I'm just sorry for you that this is the moment we're all meeting," Sarah said. When I looked up at her, I saw that her eyes were glossy.

I was grateful for their kindness and how welcoming they'd been to me, but I felt like it would be inappropriate to smile. So I tried to smile with my eyes. "Well, you didn't choose it."

"I know," she agreed. "But it's so awful. I want to ask you all the normal aunt stuff like your favorite subject in school and what you like to eat for lunch, but . . ."

"I get it," I said in a way that I hoped was encouraging.

"I have to ask, though," she said. "How's your mom?"

"Good, I think," I said.

"You think?"

I paused awkwardly. My mind scrambled for a lie, but I was too overwhelmed by the moment to come up with anything good. I managed to weakly say, "Yeah."

Sarah narrowed her eyes and made a suspicious face. I assumed it was an expression she frequently used on her students. "Taliah, does your mother know you're here?"

I didn't say anything.

"Does she?" Sarah pressed.

"Not exactly," I admitted, staring down at my hands.

Debra moved her hands away from Sarah and reached for mine. "Oh dear."

I nodded. "I know. It's bad. But she'd be mad, and I feel like we've got a lot going on as it is."

"Isn't that the truth?" Sarah muttered. And then focused her attention back on me. "But you need to tell her, okay?"

I was about to assure them that I did intend to tell Mom where I was at some point, really sooner rather than later, but before I could, Julian appeared in the hall and motioned for me to follow him.

"Go on," Debra encouraged me.

"Hey, kid," Julian said when I reached the doorway. His voice was gravelly and tired, and I know it's weird to say, but he didn't really look like a rock star to me anymore. His face was vulnerable. His eyes misty and ringed with red. He looked like a son about to lose his father. "Come on in."

An anxious feeling tightened in my chest as I stepped into the room. It was smaller than I'd expected. In the middle of the room, there was a bed with plain white sheets. Tom was lying in the bed, still and unmoving. There were several cords attached to him, and a monitor near the bed beeped occasionally in a steady and rhythmic way.

I froze near the doorway. I'd never seen someone so close to death. The drained pallor of his skin unnerved me. And his skin looked dry and was deeply wrinkled. His hands were balled in tight fists.

"'Years of survival can look awful scary,'" I said aloud without thinking. I covered my mouth. "Shit. I'm sorry."

Julian grinned sadly. "Drive-By Truckers. Fantastic band. And that song in particular is pretty great."

Something inside me eased. It was as if Julian felt it because he said, "Music, kiddo. You can't go wrong with music."

I smiled with my eyes again, and then glanced back at the bed.

"It's weird, right?" he said.

"Weird" seemed like such a flimsy way to describe it. It was weird, yes. But also so much bigger than weird.

"He drifts in and out of consciousness." Julian walked across the room and sat down on the small couch by the room's window. "When I first came in, he opened his eyes. And I think he saw me, but he didn't say anything. And then he closed his eyes again and I held his hand for a while. And the whole time, I couldn't stop wondering if he could feel it. Somehow, somewhere, you know? I just wanted that. That one simple thing. The knowledge that he could sense my presence, my flesh against his."

He patted the space next to him, and I sat.

"You don't have to be so quiet, kid. Especially since I don't think he can hear us right now. The pain medication seems to make him pretty out of it."

"Don't say that," I said.

"What?"

"Don't say that. You want this moment to count. And it should count. So don't discount it right off the bat."

Julian drew his eyebrows together. "Fair enough." He fidgeted. I could tell he'd been comforted by the idea that Tom couldn't hear him. Or wouldn't. It would break his heart later, but it had temporarily taken the pressure off him. I was starting to figure out that Julian was an emotional procrastinator.

We sat in silence for a couple of moments and then I asked, "Did you tell him about me?"

Julian nodded. "Right before I called you in here."

Tom rustled in his bed. We heard a moan and both of us startled. We leaned forward, watching him expectantly. His eyes fluttered open and a nervousness gripped my stomach. He looked right at me, and there was an awareness in his eyes that caught me off guard.

"Lena," he said, his voice a low groan.

Julian jumped to his feet. He rushed to the side of Tom's bed. "No, Dad. This is Taliah. Remember I told you about her earlier? She's Lena's daughter."

"Lena," Tom repeated weakly.

I was about to clarify that I was also Julian's daughter, a detail that seemed crucial, when Tom said, "Lena's nose." He let out a scratchy-sounding cough and then added, "Thank God."

Julian and I were silent for a moment. I looked to him because I wasn't sure how to react. It felt impossibly weird to be noticed by Tom. I didn't know if I should say something quippy back or if that would be inappropriate.

But then Julian started to laugh. He squeezed his father's hand and laughed harder, tears pooling at the corners of his eyes. "Yeah, Dad. She did get Lena's nose instead of mine. Thank God for that."

IV.

After Julian and I left Tom's room, Julian had me accompany him to the hospital cafeteria. We sat at a small round table by a large floor-to-ceiling window while Julian nursed a cup of coffee.

He wrinkled his nose as he took a sip.

"Not good?" I asked.

"Pretty stale," he said. And then, "That was something else, wasn't it?"

"Yeah," I agreed. "It was." The memory of Tom's attention hadn't left me. It was such a strange sensation to have been recognized and acknowledged by someone who up until a few days ago I had no idea existed.

"He really liked your mother," Julian offered, turning the coffee cup between his hands. Julian seemed mellower than he had been before the visit. Contemplative, even. "He thought she was a good influence on me."

I leaned forward in my chair, resting my elbows on the table. "Really?"

"Yeah. He could tell she was motivated, whereas he thought I was aimless." Julian laughed as though he were remembering something. "And he was right, I guess."

"That you were aimless?"

Julian looked straight at me. "I wasn't brave enough to admit to myself or anyone else what I wanted. Your mother changed that for me."

I stared down at the table. "But I thought you wanting to be a rock star was what upset your dad. And if Mom is the one who convinced you to really go for it, why did he like her?"

Julian ran a hand through his messy hair and gave me a little smile. "Look, Dad and I were really close when I was a kid. I was the firstborn and the son." He paused and then added, "The only son. That means something to men like my dad, you know?"

I gave him a noncommittal shrug.

"When I was younger, we used to build all sorts of cool shit in his workshop. Toy trains, airplanes. You name it. And

I loved it, and he loved that I loved it. But around ten or eleven, I grew into my own person." He met my eyes again. "Does that make sense?

"Like up until that point, I feel like I was just imitating my dad. I was interested in the things he was interested in because I wanted to be just like him. And then all of a sudden, I discovered interests of my own," Julian continued. "And my dad, he didn't handle it that well."

I nodded because I wanted him to go on.

"I think he was hurt that I wasn't interested in messing around in his workshop anymore. I actually realized I found woodworking to be super boring." Julian laughed again and shook his head. "I bought a cheap used guitar and started spending hours in my room playing covers of old punk rock songs and fooling around trying to write my own melodies. My dad *hated* the noise, and even more he hated that he thought I was wasting my time fooling around, doing aimless things. So we started to argue all the time." His eyes went hazy like he was reliving a memory. "We would snap at each other about the stupidest stuff. And we started saying worse and worse things. Before we knew it, we were locked in this cycle of resentment and silence." He shook his head again. "And I just wish I had worked to make things right before . . ."

"Yeah," I said quietly. "But you couldn't have known he was going to have a stroke."

Julian sighed. "Yeah, well, I should've known I wasn't going to have forever. But . . ." He trailed off and pinched the skin between his eyebrows, his forehead wrinkled with thought. "Life has a way of tricking you into thinking that you're always going to have forever. But this, this has snapped me out of it. And I don't want to make the same mistakes with you." He looked at me earnestly. "I've lost enough time, and I'll be damned if I'm going to lose any more."

"You could've had a whole other year," I said, half joking.

He hung his head. "I know. But I was a coward. An ashamed coward." I could tell by the way he said that that there was something else there, but before I had the chance to push it, he said, "You know, I've written a lot of songs about death. And people have loved them." He winced and his cheeks flushed red. "Sorry. I didn't mean to sound like a blowhard."

"You didn't," I volunteered. "I know what you're saying. 'Watermelons and Clocks' is one of your most popular songs."

He nodded, a sense of relief on his face. "That's 'cause people love to think about death. Or we love to think that we love to think about it. There's something almost romantic about death that sort of intrigues everyone because of the terrifying knowledge that it's coming for us all."

I stared at him blankly, not quite sure where he was going with this.

"But it's not exciting when it's like this, is it?" he said, and I could tell he wasn't really asking me, so I stayed quiet. "Like how it is with my dad? It's just sad. Really fucking sad. Slow and sad and almost boring. Isn't it awful that it's boring? That it's a morbid waiting game?" He shook his head, his lips pursed in disgust. "This shit, the real shit, it doesn't make a good song. No one wants to hear or think about this."

"I don't know," I said tentatively. "I bet you could come up with something meaningful. There are plenty of really, really sad songs that are also beautiful."

"Yeah," Julian agreed. "But now I'm not so sure how honest they are. Mine especially." He tapped his fingers against the rim of the Styrofoam coffee cup.

"But that's what I'm saying," I said, less tentatively this time. "I think your newfound honesty and awareness is what would make the song beautiful. Brutal, but beautiful."

A look crossed over his face and he gave me a tiny smile. "You're right. And you know what? You should write it."

My stomach dropped. I crossed my arms over my chest and sank down into the plastic cafeteria chair. "I don't think so," I finally said, my voice barely above a whisper.

"It was just a suggestion, since Harlow mentioned you write songs and—"

I cut him off. "Can we not talk about my songs?" I squeezed my arms tighter around myself.

He gave me a wounded look. He held his hands up in the

universal gesture for surrender. "Okay, okay. I'm sorry. It's just . . ."

I knitted my eyebrows together. "It's just what?"

"I'm sort of wondering when you're going to let me in."

I squirmed in my chair. An uneasiness that felt a little bit like anger was bubbling in my gut.

He gave me a desperate look. "Am I wrong? I just feel like since we've met, you've been holding back." His eyes searched mine. "Your mom was like that."

The uneasiness faded away as the anger took over. "And she was obviously right to be—considering what you did."

"Tal . . ."

"Do you expect me to spill my guts out to a man I hardly know? A man who hasn't been around for the entirety of my life?" I stood up from my chair. "You really have no idea." I spun on my heel and headed toward the hospital cafeteria exit.

I heard him call out from behind me. "Tal. I made a lot of mistakes, but you don't know the whole story."

I shook my head, but I didn't turn around. I kept on walking.

"Tal!" he shouted, this time louder. "I'm not the one who left."

V.

I gaped at Harlow from across the room where we'd been hanging out. It took me a moment to process what she was telling me. I couldn't believe this was happening, especially right after my argument with Julian.

"You're seriously going to leave?"

Harlow nodded. She was sitting on the end of one of the twin-size beds in Debra's guest room. "In about two hours. Julian said he could take me to the bus station before you guys eat dinner."

I flopped down on the other twin bed.

"Tal," Harlow said. "Don't be mad." She fiddled with

her elephant-shaped pendant that had been made out of a recycled spoon. Quinn had given it to her last month. Before the elephant-shaped pendant, she almost always used to wear a simple silver necklace with a tassel. I had a matching one that I still wore.

"'Mad' isn't quite the word," I said. "I feel like you're ditching me."

"I'm not ditching you," Harlow insisted. "It's just . . . I don't think you need me here anymore. This is your time. For you to be with your family. And you're going to be able to get to know them better if I'm not always around talking over you." She smiled nervously. "I know you think it's annoying when I talk over you."

I didn't say anything. I didn't want to give her the satisfaction of being even the tiniest bit right.

"Plus," she admitted sheepishly, "if I'm being honest, which I think I have to be, Quinn has a show tomorrow that I really want to make it to."

I sighed and pressed my head deeper into the pillow. "Of course. I should've guessed."

"But it's not like that," Harlow said quickly. "I would stay here if I really thought you needed me. But I don't think you do. And I actually think I'm making things worse. But you know that I would stay, right?"

"Honestly? Not really." I stared at the black-and-white photograph on the wall. It seemed to be a picture of the

Oliver house, and it was the only decorative item in the whole room, unless you counted the one simple brass lamp. Debra was clearly not an ostentatious woman.

Harlow hopped off her bed and came over to sit down next to me. "Tal. Look at me."

I glanced up at her reluctantly.

"I would stay. You know that, don't you?" she repeated.

"Actually," I snapped, "I don't. Because I just had a big fight with Julian and I definitely feel like I still need you and yet you're leaving anyway."

She sat up on her knees. "You told me it wasn't a fight. You said it was an argument."

I half laughed. "Are you kidding me? You know it was a fight. Or at least something like it."

She touched my shoulder, but I shrugged her off. "You know, Tal, I think it will be really good for you to talk with him about what he said."

I squinted at her in confusion. "Why? So I can get pissed off at him all over again? I mean, what right does he have to push me to be more open with him? Or even worse, to judge my mom?"

"I don't think he was judging your mom," Harlow said quietly. "And you have to admit, he's right. You aren't exactly an easy person to get to know."

"Yeah," I said, tossing my hands in the air. "So maybe I'm making things a little difficult for him. But don't you think I have the right to be a little suspicious of the dude? Just a tiny bit hesitant around him? I mean, where has he been my whole life? And now I'm thrown into this situation where I'm supposed to grieve a grandfather I never even met before today. So excuse me for having some emotional barriers, but I think it's justified."

Harlow chewed on her bottom lip.

"Just say whatever it is that you're thinking," I mumbled.

"It's just," she said, straightening her posture. She folded her hands onto her lap. "I think it's totally natural to have a little bit of emotional distance with Julian, but it's not just Julian, Taliah. You never let anyone new in.

"The whole time I've known you, which in case you've forgotten is since the first day of second grade, you've only ever trusted me and your mom."

"So?" I said, and leaned back against the headboard.

"Doesn't that strike you as odd?"

I made a face. "That I don't have a lot of friends?"

"No," Harlow said quickly. "Obviously you have other friends."

That was a generous thing of her to say, but not entirely true. I had other acquaintances. It's not like if Harlow and I didn't have the same lunch bell, I wouldn't have anyone to sit with, but there wasn't anyone else I told anything meaningful to. Sure, I had those people I'd chat with about my score on the pop quiz in bio or the latest episode of *True Detective* or Sufjan Stevens's new album, but it never got any deeper than that.

"You just don't . . ." She trailed off.

"Don't what?" I pressed her, even though I already knew what she was going to say.

"Really have anyone close to you other than me and your mom."

"Yeah," I admitted. "Well, it's tough. You wouldn't get that, but it is."

Harlow narrowed her eyes. "What does that mean?"

"It's just it's obviously so easy for you to trust people. You don't ever seem worried that they're going to hurt you."

"Tal," she said firmly. "Of course I worry about that. But that's life. And I think the risk is worth it."

I shrugged. "Well, good for you. But I don't know about that. And you know what? You were enough for me, even though I obviously wasn't enough for you."

Harlow shook her head. "That's so unfair."

"How, Har?" I said, raising my voice and surprising us both. "How is that unfair? Did you or did you not basically ditch me for Quinn?"

Harlow shook her head again. "Tal. I didn't ditch you for Quinn. Don't you get it? The two of you occupy different places in my heart. Just because I love Quinn now too doesn't mean that I love you any less. You seem to think that there's only a limited amount of space in your life and in your heart, and I think you need to reconsider that. Expand your world and let down your guard a little bit."

"Yeah," I argued back. "But you were my number-one person, Harlow. The person I told everything to first. And you still are. And I used to be for you, but now I'm not. Don't you get how much that sucks? How much that hurts?" I sucked in a deep breath as I felt a pressure building behind my eyes.

"But it doesn't have to be like that. It's not an either/or thing. I'm not ranking the people in my life. It's not like Quinn is first and you're second."

"Well, it feels that way." I clenched my fists. "I mean, we've stopped hanging out as much. We stopped writing our songs. Everything changed once you started dating Quinn, so I don't get how you can just sit here and pretend like it didn't."

"Fine!" Harlow shouted, and it took me by surprise. I drew my knees to my chest. "You're right. Maybe things have changed. But I'm not going to apologize for that, Tal. It's called growing up. It can't just be me and you forever and ever. That's not healthy."

I swallowed. The tears I was fighting back had left a briny taste in my throat. "It was enough for me," I repeated quietly. "And I miss it."

"Yeah," Harlow said. She gave me a pitying look that somehow felt even worse than her yell.

"But it wasn't enough for me. And it shouldn't be enough for you. You need to learn how to let other people in. It'd be good for you, Tal." She reached out for my hand. "I really do think this whole Julian thing is going to be good for you in that respect."

There was a knock on the half-opened door to the guest room.

"Yeah?" I called out.

Julian poked his head through the doorway. "Sorry to interrupt, but we've got to leave now if we're going to make it in time for Harlow to catch her bus." He looked from me to Harlow and then back again. "Is everything okay?"

"Yeah," I said, hugging my knees even harder. "Everything is really effing great."

VI.

After Harlow left, I felt more alone than ever. Julian was confused about why I didn't want to ride along with them to the bus station, but he finally let it go. The sympathetic glances they both gave me as they left were the absolute worst.

There's nothing more humiliating than feeling sorry for yourself while watching other people feel sorry for you too. So of course I spent most of the time while Julian drove Harlow to the bus station moping around upstairs, feeling sorry for myself. I was going to stay up in the guest room the whole time, until Debra called up to me, asking me to come join her in the kitchen.

Once I went downstairs, I saw the kitchen was a blur of pots and pans. The whole room was filled with a delicious scent—a mix of fresh bread and spices and fried grease. Debra's hands were coated with flour and her cheeks were smudged with some kind of sauce. She reminded me of Harlow for a moment and a sadness welled in my chest. I tried to push it aside.

"There you are," she said, grinning at me. She walked over to the stove to check on one of the pots. "Looking good, looking good," she mumbled to herself, and then turned back from the pot to me. "And how are you doing?"

I contemplated deflecting. I knew a standard "fine" would probably get me out of any uncomfortable talk. But I felt too worn down to bother with a lie. I took a seat on one of the kitchen stools, my feet dangling above the floor. "I'm not sure."

Debra breathed audibly and then whistled to herself. "I hear you, sweetheart. That's why I'm cooking. Whenever things feel overwhelming, I cook." She pulled out a cutting board and started chopping up tomatoes. "What about you?"

"Hm?"

She looked over at me, her face glowing with genuine curiosity. "What do you do when you get overwhelmed?"

I thought about it for a moment. "I play the piano. Or I sit in my room and listen to music."

She smiled a little but didn't say anything. I knew what she was thinking, though. *Julian's daughter.*

"This must be strange for you," she said. She sprinkled herbs over the fresh tomatoes.

I nodded.

"It's strange for us, too." And then she quickly said, "Not in a bad way, of course."

"I get it," I said in a way that I hoped let her know that I wasn't offended.

"You know," she said, walking back over to the stove to check on a boiling pot, "you're so much like your daddy when he was younger; he reacted the same way as you when he was overwhelmed. He'd always retreat up to his room to play the guitar after a big fight with his daddy. He'd have the volume turned up so loud it would shake the whole house."

"They fought a lot?"

Something crossed over her face. Her lips pulled into a straight line. "I'm sure he told you about all that."

"A little," I admitted.

She opened the oven door and peeked inside. "Sometimes I think the problem between the two of them was that they loved each other too much. Same with him and your momma."

I swallowed. The mention of my mother unsettled me slightly. "What do you mean?"

"Julian, he's like his daddy. He feels things strongly. And

140

sometimes that scares him. I think it makes him lash out because he's afraid of how much he's feeling. He gets distant and moody, just like his old man." She swung a pot holder over her shoulder. "But maybe I'm just another old woman making excuses for my boy and my darling husband. But it's what I like to think, so I do." She smiled with her eyes. "That's the best thing about life. You can think what you want to."

"But Julian told me that Tom and him fought a lot because they had different ideas of what Julian's life should be like. Was it the same with my mom? Did she want Julian to be someone other than he was?" Julian hadn't given me the sense that Mom didn't want him to pursue music. If anything, he'd given me the opposite impression.

Debra exhaled. She wiped her hands on her apron. "I can't really speak for your momma. But concerning Tom, I'm not sure he wanted Julian to be someone different than who he was." She paused and drew her eyebrows together. "Or maybe he did. I think the problem is that sometimes when we love someone, we see a certain version of them. And we get attached to that version. Convince ourselves that that's the only version, the true version. So for Tom, Julian was his baseball-card-and-toy-train-loving little woodworking assistant. His mini-me." She laughed at the memory and then her face went serious. "It was difficult for him to accept Julian the aimless and sometimes moody musician.

141

But I believe strongly that we all have multiple versions of ourselves. And the true test of love is learning to accept all of those versions, even when it's messy. Actually, especially when it's messy."

She ambled over to the stove, lifted the lid off the pot, and declared, "Looks like it's all cooked up." She turned off the heat. "So what I'm saying is that I think Julian and Tom got hung up on singular versions of each other. And then they told themselves a certain story about the other one. A story that wasn't necessarily false, but it wasn't the whole truth either." She shook her head. "That's one of the toughest things about love, right? The way the people we love are constantly changing and we have to learn how to accept those changes. Love isn't a constant thing, you know? It's active. It's always growing." She smiled again with her eyes. She wrung out her hands. "But what do I know? You probably think I'm just a crazy old woman rambling nonsense at you."

Before I could respond, Julian stepped into the kitchen. He lifted his nose dramatically into the air. "Something smells wonderful."

Debra playfully hit him with a dishrag. "No need to butter me up."

"I'm being honest. It smells amazing." He turned to me. "Doesn't it?"

"Yeah," I agreed. "It smells pretty great."

And it tasted even better. We sat out on the back porch and crowded around the feast that Debra had prepared. In a big wooden bowl, she'd served a salad of fresh herbs, tomatoes, and mozzarella. The shining star of the meal had been the beer-battered catfish that she'd paired with smashed red potatoes and balsamic-drizzled green beans. My favorite part though, was the endless glasses of sweet tea—sugary, lemony, and poured from a large glass pitcher.

"I think I might burst," I groaned as I shoved my plate away from me. I wanted to keep eating, but I didn't think it was physically possible for me to fit any more food inside of my stomach.

"Don't burst yet!" Debra said as she sprang up out of her chair. "We still have dessert coming."

As Debra slipped back into the kitchen, I swiveled in my chair to face Julian. I had ignored him most of the dinner, but the delicious food had radically improved my mood. "Were all your family meals like this growing up?"

Julian shook his head and laughed. "Only special occasions. But Mom did always make me beer-battered catfish for my birthdays, because it was my favorite." His eyes clouded over and he focused on the darkening sky. "It was my dad's favorite dish, too. One of the few things we had in common." He turned back to me, a sad smile on his face. "I don't think it's a coincidence it's what Mom chose to make."

I leaned back in my wooden rocker. Very aware of the fact that the seat I was sitting in had presumably been crafted by Tom. "Your mom seems to think you and Tom aren't really as different as you seem to think you are."

Julian's sad smile disappeared. He drew his eyebrows together in thought. "I feel awful, because I think my bad relationship with my dad really affected my mom." He glanced over his shoulder to make sure Debra was still in the kitchen. "My mom," he continued, "she has the biggest heart of anyone I know. She just wanted us both to be happy, and I think it broke her heart that my father and I—our paths to happiness oftentimes seemed diametrically opposed. That put her in a tricky situation." He sighed and took a sip of his iced tea. "I've always felt guilty for that. But you have to understand, my father and I hardly ever openly fought. It was more about what we didn't say. My father was a quiet man, sometimes maddeningly so."

"Is," Debra said. We hadn't realized she'd stepped out onto the porch. Her face was drained of color. She looked so much more exhausted than she had just an hour ago in the kitchen. "Your father is a quiet man, Julian. And he's still alive."

What she didn't say was: *He's still alive, for now.*

Julian bowed his head deferentially. "You're right. I'm sorry, Mom."

I got a shiver when I heard him say that. There's an

S.I.T.A. song called "Sorry, Not," where Julian famously croons, *"I'm sorry, Mom."*

It was too weird to hear it in context. To put faces and specifics to the emotion that I'd made my own. I guess that's the magic of songs. The very best ones, they let you forget that they were written by someone about something that has absolutely nothing to do with you. Instead, you bend them to your life, matching the "you" of the song with whomever you want. The songs feel so much like your pain, your love, your longing, that you forget they were born from someone else's.

"No," she quickly said, setting a silver pie dish down in the middle of the table. "I'm sorry. I just can't stop thinking about . . ."

"It's going to be okay," Julian said, but it felt like he was trying to reassure himself just as much as her. He stood up and gave Debra a tight hug. She let him embrace her but didn't quite hug him back.

She sat back down in one of the wooden rockers. She leaned back, resting her arms on the armrests. Her posture reminded me of a tired queen about to announce her army's defeat in battle. The sadness, but also the relief, that comes with the end.

"I'm sorry," Debra said. "I didn't mean to spoil the mood."

"Mom," Julian said. "You don't need to apologize."

"Please eat." She gestured eagerly toward the pie dish.

"It's pecan pie. Another one of your favorites." Then she looked at me. "And if I'm remembering correctly, your mother also loved my pie."

As Julian cut himself a large slice, he said, "She sure did."

ena and Julian quickly fell into a routine. At first, they only saw each other three times a week, but before long, they were seeing each other every day. And it still didn't feel like enough time.

Lena's cousin was concerned. It wasn't that she had anything in particular against Julian, except for the obvious—he wasn't a fellow college student, and oh yeah, he was white, not Muslim, and didn't speak a single word of Arabic.

"What does that matter?" Lena challenged her cousin one afternoon when they were sitting at the kitchen table, eating a snack of pita bread slathered with za'atar and olive oil.

"We're in America now. Doesn't it make sense that I should date an American?" Lena continued, switching from Arabic to English, and the language transition clearly caught her cousin off guard.

"You want to speak in English now?"

"It's good for us to practice."

Her cousin shoved more slices of pita in Lena's direction. "If you marry an Arab, you won't need to worry about your English."

Lena bristled. "Untrue. I live in America, regardless of whom I marry. And maybe I won't marry at all." Then she added, "Or maybe I'll marry Julian."

"Allah y'eanna." Her cousin blew on the top of her steaming cup of mint tea and sighed.

Lena stretched out on the floor of Julian's bedroom. She was resting on her stomach, fiddling with her latest project. A miniature collection of women, all carved from pinewood. She'd recently become more intrigued with woodworking after speaking with Julian's father about the craft.

She studied the miniature figurines. She liked the way they had turned out, but there was something missing.

There was no spark.

Julian slid down beside her and gently kissed her cheek. She turned to him and held out one of her figurines. "Tell me what is wrong with them."

He took the figurine from her thin fingers and rolled it between his thumbs. "She's pretty," he finally said.

"But she's not saying anything." Lena sighed and flipped over onto her back. She snatched the figurine back from him. She studied her, and then glanced at the twenty identical copies of her. There was still a surge of pride that would rise in her chest when she observed her own art. This made her feel guilty, and worse, silly even. Childish. But she couldn't help it. She was still unbelievably giddy that she was finally making art with her own two hands.

She just wished her own work wasn't also a constant

disappointment to her. She wanted to be better. There was an insurmountable gap between her ambitions and the actual product she was creating.

"Be patient," Julian said. "Keep your ears open and listen. She'll talk to you eventually." He gestured toward all the figurines. "They all will."

"How typical. The musician tells me to listen."

Julian laughed and wrapped his arms around her waist, drawing her close to him. He covered her neck with kisses. "It'll come. You just have to trust it."

"I'm not so good at trust, Oliver."

"I know."

It frustrated her endlessly that Julian was a more patient artist than she was. She'd wrongly assumed he would be more impulsive. That she would be the calm-headed and steady presence in their relationship.

When she'd first met him that one afternoon, she'd seen the fire inside of him. What she had slowly come to realize was that he kept his fire tucked away. It was always there—a steady simmer in his stomach—but he wasn't prone to the types of fitful explosions that she was. Julian worked inconsistently on his music. He still worked at the diner, not that he took that job very seriously. He would often convince her to come by in the afternoons and he would sit with her at a booth, the two of them sharing a sub-par vanilla shake, him willfully skirting his server responsibilities.

When she would ask him about his music he would say, "Lena, I'm marinating."

"Oliver," she would answer, teasingly but still with a caustic bite to her voice, "marinating is for meat."

"Be patient," he would always say, kissing the space between her bushy eyebrows.

Lena was not patient, though. She dutifully worked on her art projects in between her studies. She still hadn't dropped her premed classes. Her course load was brutal. She had long, grueling chemistry labs and hours and hours of biology homework, memorizing different organisms, mapping out the life cycles of trees.

She knew she should just quit, but quitting felt like fully untethering herself from home, from her promise to her mother. And she wasn't quite ready to do that yet.

But Julian kept pushing her to.

"*Habibi*," he would say, the Arabic word for sweetheart, which he had picked up from her. (She never bothered to explain to him that if he wanted to refer to her, he should say "*habibti*." She enjoyed the slight grammatical error. Her American boy.)

"Why are you still wasting your time with that junk that you don't care about?" Julian would ask.

When she was feeling combative and frustrated, she would snap, "Why are you still wasting your time at the diner? And when are you going to tell *your* father that you don't want to run the store?"

But when she was feeling soft and vulnerable, usually when he'd catch her studying in the early-morning light, she'd say, "Because I owe it to my mother."

"I would love to meet her," he'd say.

"I'd love that too," she'd say, and her heart would feel like it was bursting because of how true and untrue that statement was. As the months in America passed, it'd become harder and harder to conjure her mother's face. She would look at the singular photograph she'd brought with her and slowly that image—that duplicated, glossy, and fake image—became the dominant one in her mind.

She ached for Jordan. Every morning when her eyelids fluttered and she found herself in Indiana instead of in her sun-soaked stone-walled bedroom back home, her insides would throb for a moment and then she would grit her teeth and whisper quietly to herself, "The first year is the hardest." Sometimes when it was really bad, she would sit up in bed, curl her knees to her chest, press her kneecaps against her heart, and pretend she was back in Amman in that dusty, crowded apartment where she grew up. She would imagine herself sitting on the outside patio with her mother, her mother taking a long drag of a cigarette, Lena dipping a *ma'amoul* into a milky and sugary tea.

She tried to keep her pain hidden from Julian because she was embarrassed by it. As always, her greatest concern was being perceived as weak. It wasn't a coincidence that all the miniature figurines she carved had secret holes in them.

Julian didn't live with his family even though they lived in the same town. Lena found this impossibly strange.

"Your parents don't mind?" she asked.

"No. They're thrilled I'm out of the house."

She frowned. "I doubt that."

"Maybe my mom misses me a little," he admitted.

Mrs. Oliver had a warm and generous personality. Like Julian, something inside of her simply glowed. Her frank way of speaking—her country drawl—and her button nose and freckled face had all endeared her to Lena immediately. The first time she'd met Mrs. Oliver, the woman had wrapped Lena up in a big bear hug, pushing Lena's head against her bosom, and stroked her hair. "You poor thing. So far away from home."

Coming from almost anyone else, such a personal gesture at a first meeting would've put Lena off. Angered her, even. After all, how did Mrs. Oliver know how she was feeling? But somehow Lena felt that Mrs. Oliver did know. And beyond that, that Mrs. Oliver really did care.

Julian's mother frequently hosted Lena and Julian for dinner. They would join his little sister, Sarah, and Julian's father, who was almost uncomfortably quiet. Lena would try to ask him a friendly question and he would respond with a monosyllabic answer.

"How are things at the store?" she'd say, carefully spreading one of Mrs. Oliver's homemade jams across a biscuit.

Mr. Oliver would say something along the lines of "Good" or "Fine" and then ask Sarah about her day.

At first Lena had found Mr. Oliver to be rude. But as Lena grew to know Mr. Oliver better, she began to find him more endearing. Yes, he was impossibly quiet. But on the rare occasions when he did talk, she began to notice his dry sense of humor and self-deprecating wit. Like once, when she asked him about the store and he said, "We're not Ethan Allen yet, but I'll be writing to Santa again this year to ask him to grant my wish."

"Dad!" Sarah had exclaimed, looking up from her plate, which was stuffed with Debra's homemade macaroni and cheese and fried chicken thighs. "Santa doesn't grant wishes. He brings gifts."

"Same thing," Mr. Oliver had said, casting a knowing sly smile in Lena's direction.

"Plus, we're all grown, Dad. We know Santa doesn't exist," Sarah continued.

"You don't say?" he'd said, and reached over to muss up the top of Sarah's head.

"I think," Lena said once to Julian, "your father would understand if you just came out and told him. You need to stop making excuses about why you're still screwing around at the diner instead of apprenticing at his store. If you just were honest, I really think he'd understand."

Julian brushed this off. And whenever she would bring it up again, he would deflect.

"He can't handle the truth just yet," he'd say. Or: "I'm going to tell him next Christmas. Just give me some time."

When Lena had first met Julian, she'd thought that he was as solid as concrete. But the more time she spent with him, the more she discovered that, like her miniature figurines, he had hidden holes.

The first time it snowed that year, Julian drove Lena to the foot of the highest hill in Oak Falls. Together they hiked to the top and sat on a blanket Julian spread out on the frozen ground.

"It's so cold," Lena said, her teeth chattering. She was fascinated by the ghostly presence of her breath. She breathed rings into the air.

"I can't believe you've never seen snow before," Julian said. Flakes fell lightly around them, dusting their jackets, sticking to the tops of their boots.

"Once in a while it snows in Jordan. I just didn't stay long enough to witness that miracle."

Julian gave her a toothy smile. "I can be your miracle."

She snuggled even deeper into him. She still found his unbridled confidence charming.

In the distance, they watched a plane take off from the snowy tarmac. Oak Falls' airport was small and only private planes flew in and out.

"Who do you think is on that plane?" Lena asked him.

"Our future selves," he answered, grinning.

He tilted his head to the sky. "It's cool to see the planes, but I'm sad the sky's too cloudy to see any stars."

"That's okay," she said softly, and rested her head on his shoulder. "I'll wish on you."

The winter of her senior year, the acceptance letters began to arrive. It didn't take her long to settle on NYU. The plan had always been to go to New York. It was Julian, after all, who had first sold her on the idea.

"That's where everyone who wants to be someone moves," he'd told her, squeezing her hand. That squeeze an unspoken commitment. A promise.

At the time of Lena's acceptance, Julian had recently switched from working at the diner to working at Mickey's, the scene of their first date. Mikey, Julian's best friend from childhood, was the son of the owner of Mickey's. Mikey and Julian had gone to the same elementary school, been members of the same Boy Scout troop, and built and flown model airplanes together. Julian seemed pleased with his job change, and even more pleased that this change had helped to rekindle his friendship with Mikey.

Lena, though, was not pleased.

"When are you going to focus more on your music?" she would ask him. "When are you going to level with your father?"

"And when are you going to tell your mom that you aren't actually planning to become a doctor?" he'd fire back.

And maybe he was right. Maybe her anxiety about his lack of progress in his music career was amplified by her feelings of guilt about what her mother would think of her life in America. She still hadn't leveled with her mother about not wanting—and perhaps, more important, not studying—to become a doctor.

One night, when she was lying on the floppy twin mattress that served as a bed in Julian's apartment, she imagined what her mother would think if she knew how Lena was living in America. She knew she needed to tell her mother the truth, but she just couldn't bring herself to do it.

She talked to her mother twice a month for exactly fifteen minutes every time. This was before Skype and other means of communication that made long distance more bearable. Every conversation, her mother would ask, "Lena, *habibti*, are you being a good girl?"

And every time, Lena would answer dutifully, "Yes, Mama." And each time it was more and more of a lie. The guilt felt like a swamp in her chest—impossible to escape and constantly growing.

"And your studies?" her mother would inquire.

"Wonderful, Mama," she'd answer. She failed to mention that she was set to graduate in the spring, but not with a biology degree. And she definitely didn't tell her mother about her acceptance to NYU's MFA program.

She told herself she would tell the truth if her mother pushed harder. But her mother was always stoic on the phone.

She never even spoke of missing Lena. After she'd made Lena profess that she was a) being a good girl and b) studying hard, her mother used the rest of the fifteen minutes to fill Lena in on all the family gossip she was missing out on—which cousin had just given birth to a baby boy, which cousin had just gotten engaged, which uncle had just purchased a new German car.

Lena, who when she'd lived in Jordan had found that gossip inane, now lived for it. She'd cradle the phone as close as she could to her ear, as if willing her mother's voice to reach out through the phone and embrace her. Her mother would often end the call by saying something that loosely translated to "Enjoy your life in the rain." Lena knew she meant it goodheartedly—it was her mother's way of expressing just how different America seemed.

Lena once told Julian about this and he'd lit up. "That's so harsh," he'd said. "And so beautiful." A handful of years later, Julian would steal this phrase and use it for his hit song "Your Life in the Rain."

For months, Julian had actually seemed to be making progress with his band. He'd assembled a ragtag group—Lena had actually introduced him to the keyboard player, Marty St. Clair. Marty had been her lab partner sophomore year and she knew he was itching to join a band. She'd put him and Julian in touch.

The band had been practicing several nights a week and managed, thanks to their bass player, Chris, to book a gig at a local dive bar. It wasn't much. But they would be opening for a more popular campus-based band and hopefully inherit some of their fans.

Lena arrived with Julian's family. His sister, Sarah, intertwined her arm with Lena's and whispered, "Isn't this so exciting? Can you believe it?" Debra seemed equally excited, but Mr. Oliver, in typical fashion, hung in the back, quietly observing everything.

It felt like they waited forever for Julian's band to come on, standing around in a small room with a low popcorn ceiling; the room smelled aggressively of cheap beer and pot. But finally, Julian appeared on the stage. His eyes found Lena's, and he smiled.

"Hi, y'all," he said into the microphone, which Lena found weird. He'd never said "y'all" the entire time she'd known him. "I'm Julian Oliver and we're Staring Into the Abyss." There was a smattering of applause that seemed much bigger thanks to Debra's big yelp.

The band started to play and at first, everything seemed fine. Not great. But fine. But slowly, Lena could tell that something was off. The beat—it wasn't matching the pace of the lyrics. Julian would no longer look at her. His face was screwed up with frustration.

The crowd began to fidget. Everyone looking at one another as if to say, "Are they really this bad?" They all hoped the next song would be better.

It wasn't.

It was worse.

Slowly the crowd started to talk among themselves. People peeled off to gather by the bar, to wait for the next band to come on. There were a few "boos," but nothing dramatic. Later Julian would tell her that he'd wished there had been more "boos," wished it had been more dramatic. Instead of just the sad, slow unspooling that it was.

After that gig, Julian quit his job at Mickey's. He started working for his father.

"You're not quitting music, are you?" Lena would press him.

He'd shrug her off. "I'm not quitting. I'm just being realistic."

Lena swallowed her disappointment. She hadn't fallen in love with him for his realism.

So she wasn't that surprised when he told her he wouldn't be moving with her to New York right away. But she was angry.

"I can't leave my family," he said, his voice knotted with tears.

"Just tell your dad that you want to be a musician. Not a goddamn woodworker!" Lena shouted at him. Her anger was palpable. She felt like she had betrayed and abandoned her family. Why couldn't he do the same? Why couldn't he just own who he was?

"I can't, *habibi*," he said, and he fell onto the ragged old armchair that was piled high with his dirty clothes.

She knew it was him, sitting in this chair, solid as ever, but she felt like she was seeing a stranger. "Then I can't do this anymore. I'm going to New York and I never want to hear from you again."

The words unsettled her as she said them out loud. But they were more like a wish than the truth at that moment. It took her more than two months to actually leave. There would be more nights like this. Worse nights. And long, painful days. There would be shouting matches and crying and apologies.

But in the end, she did leave. She packed up her bags and boarded a plane. On the flight, she gritted her teeth and reminded herself that this move was nothing.

You've crossed an ocean before, Lena, she reassured herself. *What's a couple of hundred miles?*

VII.

"Oh," Debra said, interrupting Julian. She squeezed his shoulder and got up from her chair. I followed her eyes to see three figures moving toward us.

Aunt Sarah and two boys who looked nearly identical—same cornmeal-blond hair, glacier-blue eyes, angular faces, and willowy build—pulled open the screen door and stepped onto the back porch.

"Brady! Carter!" Debra said, and raced over to them, scooping them up into one big bear hug.

"Hi, Nana," they said unenthusiastically.

"Sorry to just pop in on you like this," Sarah said. She touched her hair self-consciously.

"Don't be silly, sweetheart," Debra said. "You guys are welcome anytime." She gestured toward the table. "Take a seat! I made pie."

Sarah tumbled into one of the wooden rockers and the boys also sat down, albeit reluctantly.

"The boys wanted to come over and see you, Mom," Sarah volunteered. "And of course they wanted to see their uncle and their newfound cousin." She smiled at me.

They both kept staring at me, a sour expression on their faces. Despite what Sarah said, I was getting the distinct impression they hadn't been that eager to see me or Julian. We all sat there in awkward silence. Debra served the boys a large slice of pie each, and they slowly dug into their respective slices.

In between bites of pie, one of the twins looked at me and said, "Don't you feel weird?"

"Me?" I said, my voice a little squeaky. I stared at my feet.

"Carter," Aunt Sarah hissed. "Be nice."

"I mean," the other boy said, as if continuing for Carter, "you never even knew Grandpa."

"Brady," Sarah hissed again. "Knock it off. Where are your manners?"

"It's okay," I said quickly, looking at Sarah and then at

Julian. Julian gave me a reassuring nod. "They're right, after all. I didn't know him."

"Sweetheart, you met him today," Debra said, standing back up from her chair and walking to stand behind me. She squeezed my shoulders.

"Yes, she did," Julian said. "And we're here now. We both are." He gave me an encouraging smile.

"A little late," Carter mumbled under his breath. He shoved a forkful of pie into his mouth.

I'd expected Sarah to let out another exasperated sigh, reprimanding Carter, but instead we all turned our heads toward the porch door. Toby, the boy from this morning, was standing in the doorway sheepishly.

"Hi," he said, and gave a little wave.

"Toby!" Debra said. She greeted Toby with a hug. She cradled his face in her hands and gave him a kiss on each cheek. "What brings you over here?"

Toby leaned against the side wall of the porch. I envied how relaxed he seemed. His eyes found mine. I snuck into my seat as I felt everyone else look at me.

"The twins texted me to say they were coming over. And I thought I'd stop by and see everyone," Toby said. He slid one hand into the pocket of his jeans.

"Are we still going to go down to the lake?" Carter asked. He shoveled the last of his pie into his mouth and finished it in three large chomps.

Toby turned toward Sarah. "Would that be okay? We'd thought it might be fun to walk down to the lake Tom loved so much. If it's easier for you, the boys can spend the night at my place and I can drive them back to your house in the morning."

"Nonsense," Debra said, waving her hands in the air. "They can stay here. You all can. Sarah, why don't you call Todd and let him know you guys will be home in the morning."

"Mom, are you sure?" Sarah asked. Her voice revealed hesitance but her face showed relief. She wanted to stay here. At her childhood home. And that was perfectly understandable to me.

"But . . ." I saw a look of concern flash across Brady's face. Presumably I was staying in the room the boys always stayed in when they slept over.

Debra waved again. "Don't you worry about it. I have enough space for everybody."

"So the lake it is?" Toby said, wriggling his eyebrows in a goofy way that would've seemed gross on about 99 percent of the world's population but somehow worked for him.

"Taliah," Debra said. "Why don't you join the boys at the lake?"

Toby's face changed from goofy to almost challenging. He gave me a dare of a smile. "Yeah. How about it?"

I glanced at Julian, and our conversation from earlier that afternoon came flooding back to me. And my fight with Harlow. I was about to say no, but something inside me made me pause.

"Sure," I said pointedly. "Why not?"

VIII.

"What was that back there? Between you and Julian?" Toby asked me once we were outside. The twins ran ahead in front of us. We walked down the hill toward the wooded part of the property. The light from the Olivers' porch illuminated the swath of grass in front of us, but I knew the closer we got to the woods, the darker it was going to get.

I grimaced a little. I was surprised Toby had even noticed. "Forget about it."

"What if I don't want to forget about it?" His tone was light.

"It's dumb."

"I doubt that," he said.

"No. It really is."

"Try me?"

"I'd rather not."

"Come on. Try me."

"You're rather persistent. Has anyone ever told you that?"

"Don't switch the question around on me. I know that trick."

I sighed.

"Come on. What's going on?"

I wrinkled my nose. "Fine. So Julian was just on my case earlier today about not letting him in. He accused me of, I don't know, putting up some kind of emotional wall."

"Do you?"

"Excuse me?"

"Do you put up emotional walls?"

"Holy hell, dude," I said. "Are you like the Diane Sawyer of Oak Falls?"

In the dim light, I saw Toby's cheeks redden. There was a long pause, and I worried for a moment that I had offended him. "Naw," Toby finally said. "Not really. I'm actually not usually one for questions."

"Could've fooled me."

He grinned. "I'm full of surprises. You'll see."

I smiled back weakly and followed him down a narrow dirt path that cut sharply down a hill. By now, the Oliver porch light was just a twinkle behind us. Up above, the moon glowed—a perfect shining sliver. The air smelled like summer—botanical, lush, and thick.

"So aren't you going to ask me?" he said as we climbed farther and farther down the hill.

"Ask you what?"

"Why I'm so interested in asking you questions if it's out of my nature to do so?"

I swatted at a mosquito that I felt nibble on my left wrist. "I'm still not sure I believe you that it's out of your nature."

He laughed. "Trust me. It is."

When I didn't say anything, he let out a whistle. "Dang."

"What?"

"You're a tough cookie, you know? Your pops and your friend might be right about you."

It was my turn to blush. "You don't know me well enough to say that. Though you probably have already judged me." I gestured farther up the path where the twins were charging through the forest. "You know they already have."

Toby walked closer to me and nudged his shoulder against mine. "Aw. You misjudge them."

"They seem to hate me."

Toby shook his head, another wide grin spreading across his lips. "You don't get it."

"Enlighten me?"

"They're nervous around you," he explained. "Actually, I

think the word I'm looking for is 'intimidated.'"

"Bullshit."

Toby braced. "Whoa. Do you kiss your mother with that mouth?"

I looked at him. "You have to be kidding me."

"What?" He gave me a sheepish shrug. "I just think there are more interesting words to use."

"Really? Like what?"

"Like *pamplemousse*," he said. "It means 'grapefruit' in French. Isn't that fantastic?"

"*Pamplemousse*," I repeated, botching the pronunciation. "That's really what you say when you get pissed off?"

Another sheepish shrug. "Sure. Why not?"

"Um, I don't know," I said. "Because it doesn't make any sense."

"Sure it does. It's a fun word. So whenever I say it, I instantly feel better. Which makes deploying it in upsetting situations a win-win."

"Whatever you say," I said, nearly tripping over the exposed root of a tree.

Toby reached out to steady me. "We're getting close. Don't worry."

"I wasn't worried."

"Okay." And then added, repeating me, "Whatever you say."

I smiled despite myself.

"How do you know my cousins so well?" I asked.

"Oh," Toby said. "So now you get to ask questions?"

"Well," I said, "I think I have the right to be curious about my family that up until about forty-eight hours ago, I had no idea existed."

"No idea?" Toby said. "Really?"

"No idea," I confirmed. I gave him the brief SparkNotes version of The Shoebox discovery, and Julian showing up on my doorstep, and what Julian had told me so far about my mother and him.

"But it's not adding up," I said. "What he's told me so far makes it seem like Mom's the one who broke things off."

"And that surprises you?" Toby asked.

"Hell yes, it surprises me."

Toby braced again.

"You have to be freaking kidding. You consider 'hell' a swear word?"

He shrugged. *"Pamplemousse,"* he said with a smile. "But why does it surprise you that much?"

"Um," I said. "Because Julian's a rock star. And my mom is my mom."

"So?"

"So?" I echoed back to him. "So it just seems obvious to me that Julian ditched her when he got famous."

Toby gave me a look.

"What?"

"I dunno if you should be so sure about that. Even rock stars can get dumped, you know?"

I smiled a little. "And you're an authority on that?"

"Maybe," he said, turning his attention away from me and toward the sound of splashing in the distance. Toby grabbed for my hand and steered me down the last part of the path. The overgrown grass had given way to brush and tall trees. It was getting harder and harder to see, but Toby seemed to know the path by heart.

When we finally reached the lip of the lake, Toby announced, "Here we are." And then he unbuttoned his shirt and peeled off his pants as if that was the most natural thing in the world to do. His pale, freckled skin stood out against the darkness as he ran into the water. I watched as the bony knobs of his spine disappeared beneath the dark surface of the lake.

The twins yelped with excitement and one of them splashed Toby right in the face. He shook his head, spitting out water and laughing.

"Come on in!" he called out. "The water is great!"

I studied the lake. It was small and oddly shaped. The left side was much wider and it appeared to taper off on the right side into a tiny stream. The water had a musky scent. Not rotten, or even bad, but potent all the same.

"Come on!" Toby repeated. He was bobbing up and down.

"I don't have a swimsuit."

"She's too prissy for this," Carter said. "Just let her be."

I sat down at the edge of the lake and dipped my toe in. "That's not fair. I just don't have a swimsuit."

"You big-city girls are too good for swimming?" Brady teased as he treaded water.

I dipped my toe farther into the water. "I'm not from the big city."

"Why doesn't Julian ever come home?" Carter asked, and his voice for once didn't sound mean or teasing. It sounded like he really wanted to know. And I could swear I even sensed some hurt in there too. Like he took it as a personal offense that his uncle didn't make it home for every Thanksgiving and Christmas.

"I don't know," I stammered, and stared at the dark water in front of me.

"And we're really supposed to believe that?" Carter said, and some of the mean had snaked its way back into his voice. "He's your dad."

"Yeah," I said. "I guess technically. But I hardly know the guy."

"Us either," Brady said.

"So that's something we have in common." I gave them a weak smile, which neither of them returned, but out of the corner of my eye, I saw Toby watching me.

Toby splashed his arms in the water and repeated, "Come on in."

"I would, but I don't have a swimsuit."

"So?" Carter said. "Neither do we. Just swim in your underwear."

"But . . ."

"Don't be weird," Brady said. "We're family."

A fuzzy feeling bubbled in my stomach. "Family, huh?"

"Yeah." Carter affirmed his brother's statement. "Family."

Toby splashed his arms again. "Hey, I'm not family. But I promise not to look." He swam in a circle, turning his back to me.

"Don't be a perv, Toby," Carter groaned, and Brady laughed.

I took a deep breath and then quickly slipped my T-shirt up over my head. I unbuttoned my jeans and stepped out of them. I ran into the water and landed with a splash.

"That landing proves you're family," Carter said to me.

I gave him a fake salute. "Glad to have proved myself."

"Don't get too high on yourself yet," he warned. "I said it proved you're family. I still haven't decided if I like you."

Brady laughed and splashed his brother.

"So you guys used to come here a lot with Tom?"

All three of them nodded.

"He always wanted to fish out here," Carter said with a laugh. "But we never caught any fish."

"But those afternoons were the best," Brady filled in. "Nana would pack us sandwiches and we'd sit out here for hours with Grandpa. Swimming and joking around." A look passed over Brady's face. "Remember when Toby pretended to be a fish that one day?"

They all doubled over laughing.

"When Gramps wasn't looking," Carter explained to me, "Toby would dive under and tug at his bait."

I was getting the sense that Toby pretty frequently made a fool of himself to entertain the twins, but he didn't seem that eager to go over every one of his efforts. "It was funnier when we were younger," he said, and something about his voice made me think he was blushing again.

"Let's play chicken!" Brady said.

Carter pretended to groan. "Gramps hated chicken."

"Exactly," Brady said. "So it's the perfect way to honor him."

"By doing something that would definitely piss him off?" Carter said.

"What could be more perfect?" Toby chimed in. "The old man was always pissed."

"That he was," Brady agreed.

"In the best sort of way," Carter said, and I could hear the emotion in his voice.

"So what do you say, newbie?" Brady asked me. "You and Toby versus Car and me?"

I looked to Toby and he gave me a reassuring smile. "Yeah," I said. "I'm in."

IX.

The walk back was similar to the walk there. Except that we were all soaked. The ends of my hair kept dribbling water onto my T-shirt. The twins darted ahead of us, but Toby lagged behind with me.

"See?" he said. "They're not so bad."

"I never said they were bad," I argued. "I said that they hated me."

"They seem to hate you a tiny bit less now," Toby offered.

"Probably because of my exceptional chicken skills," I said.

"Probably," he agreed.

We walked in silence for a few moments and then I said, "I wish I'd come to Oak Falls sooner."

Toby let out a deep breath. "I wish you had too."

"Hey," I said. "Earlier you said you weren't really one for questions. But you kept asking me questions. Why?"

He bumped his shoulder against mine. "Because I find you interesting."

I swallowed and tried to ignore the flipping sensation in my stomach. "You don't even know me."

"That's true," he conceded. "Or at least not well."

"So how do you know I'm interesting?"

He grinned. "At first, I was interested in you because your story was interesting. Girl meets famous father and his family after all these years? After Carter and Brady filled me in on your existence, I knew I had to check you out."

"Check me out?" I teased.

He laughed. "You know what I mean."

"So you had an eye out for me this morning?"

"Yeah," he admitted. "I'd been prepared to dislike you, actually."

"Because of Carter and Brady?"

"Sort of," he said. "And because I was jealous that you were actually related to Tom."

"But you were the one that actually knew him."

He gave me a wry look. "I didn't say my thinking was rational. Tom meant a lot to me."

I swallowed and worked up the nerve to ask the question that had been on my mind. "Because of your own father?"

"Yeah," Toby said slowly. "This will probably sound silly to you, but I really wanted Tom's respect because I knew my dad had deeply respected Tom. And if I wasn't ever going to have the chance to prove myself to my dad, the next best thing I could do was prove myself to Tom."

"I'm sorry," I blurted out.

His face registered surprise. "For what?"

"I've been whining about my dad and, well, it's complicated, he's . . ."

"Alive?" Toby filled in.

"Yeah," I said softly.

He nudged my shoulder again. "Don't worry about it. I know you big-city girls think you're all-powerful, responsible for every choice the Universe makes and all that, but you aren't responsible for my dad's death. Or the fact that your dad is still alive." He pointed up at the sky. "That's beyond even you, you know?"

My shoulder tingled in the spot where he had briefly touched it. I followed his finger to the sky, taking a moment to revel in the brightness of the stars. Looking up at them made me feel impossibly small, in the best sort of way. "I told you already, I'm not from a big city."

"I know," he said, smiling. "It's just fun to tease you."

I shook my head, laughing a little. "Does that mean

you've revised your opinion of me from this morning?"

"This morning? I changed my mind the moment I saw you."

We stepped out of the woods into the clearing. The shadowy outline of the Oliver farmhouse hovered in the distance.

"That's not true," I said softly, not completely trusting my voice.

He touched my arm lightly. "Yes, it is. I saw you this morning and I . . ." He trailed off for a moment.

"And you . . . ?"

He rubbed the back of his neck. "I'm trying to think of how to say this in a way that will make sense."

I stayed quiet, waiting.

"This morning, I saw you walking along this fence." He gestured to his side where the white equestrian-style fence was, dividing the Oliver property from his own. "And I recognized something in you."

"Recognized?"

"Yeah. Something about you felt so familiar. I don't know why, but . . ." He pulled at the hem of his shirt. "But I want to," he finished, leveling his eyes with mine.

I found myself bracing. I'm not sure why. It's a funny thing how excitement, like hope, can feel a whole lot like fear. "You mistook me for someone else?"

"No, silly," he said, and his voice was gaining strength. "I recognized something in you. There was something about the way you were walking."

"What about it?" I pressed. "My terrible posture?"

He laughed. "No."

"Then what?"

He shook his head. "It'll sound dumb."

"Try me."

"You seemed lost and found at the same time. And that's how I usually feel too."

X.

It was late when we got home. I said a quick good night to the twins and then padded up the stairs. I tiptoed into the guest bedroom and flopped down on my bed. It seemed lonely in the room without Harlow.

If she had still been here, I probably would've crawled into her bed and laid next to her—head to head, toe to toe, like how we used to do when we were little. When Har first came out in eighth grade, some idiots relentlessly teased me. They asked if I was worried that Harlow would creep on me while I changed or crawl into my bed in the middle of the night during sleepovers—all of which were obviously ridiculous concerns. Anyone who knew us would've known I was the one always crawling into Harlow's sleeping bag, as I was the one who had night terrors. (Not to mention, if I were gay, Harlow would've been way out of my league.)

But she wasn't here anymore, so I rolled onto my side and tried to go to sleep. But I couldn't. I took a deep breath and reached for my phone. I dialed Harlow's number.

After three rings, I was almost certain she wasn't going to answer.

But after the fourth ring, she picked up. "Tal?"

"Yeah," I said. "Did you get home okay?" I could hear people chatting in the background and I wondered where she was.

"Yeah. But how are you?"

"Weird," I said. "Really weird. And I'm still pissed at you."

There was a long pause. For a moment, I wondered if Harlow had hung up. But then I heard breathing—a series of long exhales. I imagined her pacing across a room.

"I know," she finally said.

"I don't want us to grow apart."

"I know," she repeated. "I don't want that either."

"But sometimes it feels like you do."

"I just want us to both have the chance to grow. To change. But that doesn't have to mean growing apart," she said.

I thought of what Debra had told me about love being a living and changing thing. About how the tricky thing was learning to accept different and new versions of the people you loved. The problem was that it seemed like I was never the one who changed. It seems like it's harder to watch the people you love change and grow when you feel like you're staying exactly the same. When you feel stuck.

But maybe tonight I had changed. Even if it was only a tiny bit.

"You'll never guess what happened tonight," I said.

"What?" she said, and I could hear the curiosity in her voice. That made me smile. So I told her all about the lake and the slight progress I'd made with the twins. And Toby.

"Wait," she said when I was finished. "You guys didn't kiss?"

I laughed. Of course that was Harlow's first question. "Nope. Plus, it would've been too weird anyway. It feels like the wrong timing."

She made a noise.

"What?"

"I thought you were going to work on giving more new people a chance?"

"I am!" I protested. "I went to the lake, didn't I? And you would've been so proud of me. I actually talked to him. About real things. I hardly recognized myself. Like, Har, I answered his questions. Personal questions."

"I am proud of you," she said, and I smiled to myself in the darkness of the room. "But seriously. No kiss?"

"Harlow! It's the wrong time. And the wrong place."

"What's so wrong about Oak Falls? 'Nothing, like something, happens anywhere.'"

My smile widened. Harlow was quoting the Philip Larkin poem "I Remember, I Remember," which she and I dissected last year in English class. She'd loved that line, and I'd thought it was stupid and nonsensical because it was so obvious.

But maybe what Harlow got then is what I'm starting to understand now—that it's sometimes the most obvious things that need to be said the most.

"Hey, Har?"

"Yeah?" she said.

"I'm glad you came with me. Even if I'm still mad at you for leaving."

"I'm glad I came too," she breathed.

"We're going to be okay, right?"

There was a long pause on her end. I thought for a moment we had been disconnected, but then she finally said, "Yeah, Tal. We're going to be okay."

There was another stretch of silence and then she said, "Before we hang up, I need you to do something for me."

"What?"

"I want you to call your mom."

"What?" I sat up with force and clutched the phone tightly.

"Please, Tal. I'd feel better if you called her. Besides, you promised me that you'd call her once we got to Oak Falls."

"And you promised that you'd stay with me. And you didn't," I shot back.

"No. I. Did. Not," she argued. "I said I would come with you on what I thought was an ill-advised trip, but have since come around to thinking otherwise." And then she quickly added, "But I haven't changed my opinion on the fact you need to call your mom."

"Ugh," I repeated.

"Tal, you should call her now. Just get it over with."

"Can't it wait until tomorrow morning?"

"Just do it now," Harlow pleaded.

"I don't even know what time it is in Paris. She's probably just waking up. Or busy."

"That's a flimsy excuse and you know it."

I slouched back down, resting my shoulders against the headboard. "I don't know, Harlow. The truth is, the more Julian tells me, the more I wonder if I don't really know my mom as well as I thought I did. Like tonight, I found out she was the one who first ended things. Can you believe that?"

Harlow made a surprised sound.

"See?" I pressed. "It's weird."

"Yeah. All the more reason why you should call her. You

haven't given her a chance to tell you her side of the story."

"She only had sixteen years," I pointed out.

"I'm sure she had her reasons," Harlow said diplomatically. For all her punk rock bravado, she still had a deep respect for authority figures.

"Maybe I could just email her. She doesn't like to pay international premiums."

"Taliah. Stop messing around. And call her. Please."

"Fine," I said.

"Text me once you've done it?"

I agreed reluctantly and hung up on Harlow. I scrolled through my contacts and selected Mom. She had a paintbrush emoji next to her name. I assigned all my contacts corresponding emojis. For a moment, I let myself wonder about whether I would ever have Julian's number and what emoji I would select for him.

I pressed Call and brought the phone to my ear. I listened to it ring and hoped beyond hope that Mom was asleep and she'd turned her ringer on silent. When I heard the sound of her automated voice informing me that I'd reached Lena Abdallat's voicemail, I breathed a sigh of relief.

At the beep, I left my message: "Mom, it's Tal. So don't freak out, everything's okay. I'm safe and healthy and everything, but there's something I need to tell you. And it seems wrong to be telling you this over voicemail but . . ." I trailed off, my nerves getting the best of me.

I swallowed, gathering my courage, and continued, "You'll never guess who showed up on our doorstep. Julian Oliver. Yeah. So the thing is . . . well . . . a while ago . . . You know what. Never mind. I'll explain the details later. But I just wanted to let you know that I'm in Oak Falls with Julian. Tom had a stroke and he's really sick and they think he might die, so Julian wanted to come back home. Tom is Julian's dad. Wait. You know that already. Okay . . . well, this is getting really weird and—"

The automated voicemail robot was back. I elected to save my rambling message, and then hung up the phone.

DAY THREE

(In Which I Learn That a Pause Is Sometimes a Way of Holding On)

I.

n the morning I was waiting for Julian to come downstairs when Debra caught me eyeing the piano.

"That's right," she said. "You know how to play." I'd woken up before anyone else. The twins were presumably still asleep and Aunt Sarah was in the shower. When Julian had woken up, he'd knocked on my door to make a plan for the day, and I guess Debra had heard us talking because she materialized in the kitchen to brew a pot of coffee.

"Will you play something for me?"

I hesitated. I glanced down at the piano. It was exactly the style of piano I would've guessed Debra would own. It was simple and made of solid dark wood that showed its age and had a couple of scratches. It was nothing fancy, but the keys were in perfect condition.

"Did Julian ever play?"

Debra laughed lightly. "Julian was never that into the piano. He told me it was a church instrument. He was always much more interested in the guitar."

I smiled. "Sounds like him, I guess."

"So, will you?" Debra prompted. "Play me something?" She sat down on the love seat that was adjacent to the piano.

I swallowed. "What would you like me to play?"

"Anything," she said cheerfully, tossing her hands in the air. "I'm not picky." But then she added, "Do you write your own songs? If so, I'd like to hear one of those."

I squirmed on the piano bench. "I don't know." My fingers hovered over the keys. "I've never written anything that special. And everything is really rough."

"Taliah?" Debra said, and I looked up at her.

"Yeah?"

"I'm your grandma. Not a music critic. Please just let me hear one of your songs."

I laughed a little. "That might be true, but you're Julian Oliver's mom, so that's sort of intimidating."

She waved me off. "Hogwash." And then she dipped her chin to her chest and leaned toward me in a conspiratorial way. "To be honest," she whispered, "I've never understood

Julian's music. I love it because he made it and I love him with my whole heart, but I don't have the ear to understand what makes it so special." She paused, and then smiled broadly. "Tom did, though. Tom would listen to all of Julian's songs and analyze them piece by piece."

My eyes widened. "Really? I thought Tom hated Julian's music."

Debra shook her head. "No, no. That was one of the huge misunderstandings between them. I think Tom may have resented Julian's music when he was younger, but he loved all of Staring Into the Abyss's records. Actually . . ." She trailed off, a look of sadness washing over her face. "Right before his stroke, he'd asked me if I knew when the band planned to release a new record."

"Really?" I repeated.

"Truly," she said. "It's been a while since they've released a new album now, hasn't it?"

"Yeah. There's a lot of pressure on them."

Her face had a quintessential worried mom expression. "Hopefully not too much pressure."

"I'm sure Julian can handle it," I assured her.

"So, your songs," she insisted. "Please play me one of them."

I don't know if it was because Debra had just revealed that Tom was a secret fan of S.I.T.A. or what, but I felt something open up in me. I volunteered, "Okay, so the only original songs I have are ones I wrote with Harlow."

Debra nodded.

"I wrote the music," I explained. "And we would write the lyrics together and then Harlow would sing while I played the piano."

Debra nodded again. "Sounds lovely. I've always been partial to girl bands." She gave me another conspiratorial tilt of her head. "Don't tell Julian."

"Your secret is safe with me," I said, smiling. "But the thing is, Harlow . . . well . . . she . . ." I paused for a moment because I wasn't sure how open my long-lost grandma was to lesbian relationships. I decided to try Debra. "You see, Harlow recently started dating this girl Quinn."

"Oh," Debra said. Her eyes registered surprise, but she said, "Go on."

"And Quinn," I explained, "is much cooler than me. And I think Harlow started to feel that our little music project was nerdy because Quinn is in, like, a real band. A very scene band if you know what that means."

Debra gave me a thoughtful smile. "Not sure I do exactly, but I think I follow."

I felt my cheeks warm. "Sorry. I don't know why I'm telling you all of this."

"Baby girl," Debra said, stretching her arm out so she could gently squeeze my shoulder, "I want to hear anything you're willing to tell me."

I bit my lip. "I guess what I was trying to explain is the song I'm about to play might sound a little weird. Like it's missing something since Harlow isn't here to sing the lyrics." I glanced up at the ceiling and sighed. "I guess that's been the whole problem. I'm going to have to figure out how to write songs without Harlow that don't feel like they're missing something."

"Well," Debra said encouragingly, "let's hear one of these songs."

I readjusted my seat on the bench, placing my feet squarely on the floor. I took a deep breath and placed my fingers on the keys. I decided to play a song Harlow and I called "Snow Drifts." It had partially been inspired by Arcade Fire's song "Neighborhood #1 (Tunnels)." We wanted to capture the same type of romantic whimsicality. But the song was also a little bit jazzier, a nod to the punk cabaret that we were aiming for.

We'd written the song on a snow day. It had been a long, lazy day, full of bottomless mugs of hot chocolate and lounging around in pajama pants. I smiled as I got into the meat of the song, remembering how comfortable and easy that day had been.

I played the last few notes and looked up to see Debra watching me intently. Tears were glistening in her eyes.

"Was it that bad?" I said meekly.

She laughed a little as she blew her nose with a tissue.

"Don't be silly, sweetheart. That was beautiful. I just . . ." She stopped talking, her eyes zeroing in on the other side of the room.

I turned around to see Julian standing at the edge of the foyer. His arms were crossed and he was leaning against the staircase's railing. I rubbed my forearms self-consciously and scooted down the piano bench. "Oh. I didn't realize you were here."

"I snuck in when I heard the piano. And I'm so glad I did."

We all froze there for a moment in uncomfortable silence. It was one of those times where I knew we all wanted to say something, but words seemed to be lacking. It seemed impossible to say what we really wanted to say. We could've tried to construct elaborate metaphors or pithy condolences and compliments, but none of them would get to the heart of the matter. So instead, we all stood there, feeling the moment instead of speaking about it.

And somehow that felt like enough.

"Should we go?" Julian finally asked.

I nodded, and as we walked out the door, Debra called out, "Hey, Taliah?"

"Yeah?" I said, turning my head.

She flashed me a mischievous smile. "Your song didn't sound like it was missing anything. Not a damn thing."

II.

Julian took one hand off the steering wheel and pointed to the left. "See that hill over there?"

I craned my neck and saw a noticeably tall hill off in the distance. "Yeah."

"That's the hill I told you about earlier. The one your mom and I used to climb when we were younger. It overlooks the tarmac of Oak Falls's local airport. Hardly any flights come in and out of there, only personal planes. We used to pretend that someday we'd have a private plane that would take us far away from Oak Falls."

He turned the car and the hill faded into the distance. "A

while ago, I actually did land in a private plane here. When the plane hit the tarmac, I looked up at that hill and almost lost my shit."

"Why?"

"Because Lena wasn't next to me."

An itchy feeling crept up my throat and I swallowed. I stared out the window in silence for the rest of the drive.

Julian parked the car on a curved, tree-lined street populated with small cafés and independent shops. He hopped out of the car and I followed him into a store called Willowy Records.

"Willowy Records," I said as we walked into the small, cramped space filled with rows and rows of vinyl records. A small fan was doing overtime in the back corner, but it did little to remove the musky scent or make the place less unbearably hot.

"Best record shop in Oak Falls." Julian reached for his sunglasses, but it was too late. The scrawny boy behind the counter leapt over it and marched toward him.

"Holy shit!" the kid exclaimed. He had dyed black hair that was shaved on the sides and mussed up in the front. His gray T-shirt, which featured an octopus playing the drums, had several sweat patches, but that was forgivable considering the tropical climate of Willowy Records. "You're Julian Oliver."

"Guilty as charged," Julian said calmly.

"I'd heard you were in town, man," the boy said, clasping his hands together. "But I didn't quite believe it."

Julian nodded.

The boy bowed his head a little. "So sorry about your dad."

"Me too," Julian said. "So listen . . ."

"Mark," the kid said, extending his hand. "I'm Mark."

Julian shook his hand. "Nice to meet you, Mark."

"Such an honor, man. Your music. Dude. *Dude.*" Mark made the universal gesture for "mind blown," miming explosions. "It totally changed my life. Such a huge fan of every album. But especially *Blind Windows.*" Mark's eyes lit up. "Would you be willing to sign a few of your records while you're here, man? That would be huge for the store."

Julian nodded. "Sure, man. But let me tell you what. I'm here right now with my daughter." Julian unexpectedly slung his arm around my shoulder and tugged me close to him. "And I'd like to have some private time browsing some records with her. So do you think you could hold off on posting anything on—"

"Yeah, yeah," the kid said, enthusiastically nodding his head, which seemed too big for his thin neck. "Def won't post anything yet, man. You enjoy your time. And when you're done—"

"I'll sign those records," Julian said without missing a beat.

"Yeah," the boy said, still nodding. "Awesome."

Julian kept his arm around me and steered me away from the front of the store. "Sooo, where do they keep the jazz records?"

I groaned. "I don't only listen to jazz, you know."

"I know," he said agreeably. "So are all the songs you write jazz-inspired?"

An uncomfortable nervousness stirred inside of me. "I thought you said you liked my song. And that one wasn't even that jazzy. It actually had more of an indie rock sensibility, I think."

"I know. I did love it. It actually reminded me of—"

I cut him off. "Can we not talk about it? I'm really not ready to talk about my music with you."

"Fine, fine." He raised his hands innocently in the air. "Can I at least ask you about other music you like?"

"Besides Nina Simone?" I gave him a teasing smile.

"Yeah. I mean, if you like anything else."

"So bands that I like that you might've heard of . . ." I slid out from under his arm and walked down the aisles of records. I stopped and thumbed through a stack. I held up the National's *High Violet*.

"Ah." Julian nodded in recognition.

"Have you heard of EL VY?"

Julian drew his eyebrows together and wrinkled his nose. "I think so . . ." He rhythmically tapped his fingers against his leg. "That's Berninger's side project, right?"

"Yeah. It's him and Brent Knopf, the guy from Menomena," I said, fishing through the bin to see if I could find a copy of *Return to the Moon*.

"Didn't *Pitchfork* recently eviscerate that album?"

I laughed. "Yeah. But I love it. But I was destined to love it. He's singing about southern Ohio." I found the record and held it up. "Plus, what does *Pitchfork* know? Didn't they tear apart *You'll Never See Me Again*?"

Julian let out a bark of a laugh. "Yeah, kid. They did. But let's not talk about that."

I fingered the EL VY record and then put it back in the bin. "I thought you didn't read the reviews?"

He smiled wryly. "That was my last one."

"It was also your last record. So when's the next one coming out?"

He laughed again. "Why do you care? I thought you weren't a fan."

I shrugged. "I dunno. It's been a long gap between albums, and lots of people on the internet have been speculating about when the next one will drop. Besides, I'm kind of interested in the band because I know the lead singer."

His smile turned from wry to bright. "Yeah. I guess you do. So besides the genius of S.I.T.A., who else are you into?"

I gave him my usual litany of indie darlings—Joanna Newsom and her amazing stylings on the harp and Kurt

Vile and his hyper-self-aware songwriting. I nervously rattled off Deerhunter and Beach House and Father John Misty. Julian said that as much as he appreciated modern indie rock music, his favorites would still always be classic punk bands and David Bowie. But as far as indie rock music was concerned, he agreed with me that Stephin Merritt of the Magnetic Fields was a genius at tragicomedy, but he said that he thought Sufjan Stevens was overrated, which was basically a declaration of war as far as I was concerned.

"You're just jealous that he not only is a world-class song-writer, but also has a perfect face."

"Maybe," Julian admitted sheepishly.

"Harlow and Quinn are really into this goofy band called the Front Bottoms. You might like them. I bet you'd get the humor." I moved down another aisle in search of *Talon of the Hawk*. Once I found it, I turned around and held it up for Julian to see.

He took the record from me and ran his thumb over the cover. He was quiet for a moment, studying the record with such intensity that I wondered if maybe I'd overhyped the band.

"They're pretty fun," I offered. I was starting to feel a little insecure about my suggestion, so I added, "Like I said, Harlow loves them."

He looked up at me. There was a new intensity in his eyes. "You love music, right, Taliah?"

I bit the inside of my lip. "Of course. But isn't saying that like saying I enjoy breathing oxygen? I've never met someone who didn't like music."

"But you love it, right? Like really love it?" he pressed, his eyes still intense. I broke away from his gaze and pretended to be interested in browsing through the records.

"Sure," I said.

"What do you love about it?"

"What do *you* love about it?" I flipped the question back around on him.

"Everything," he said.

"That's a cop-out."

"Okay. Well, for starters, I love the way music holds and enhances our memories. Certain songs can always transport me right back to particular moments in my life. It's like magic."

I pulled out a Sun Kil Moon record from the bin. "Your own songs?"

He shook his head. "No. Not really. Sure, I've cataloged my life by my own songs, but I'm talking about other people's music."

"Give me an example."

He ran a hand through his messy hair. "Whenever I hear Neutral Milk Hotel's 'Where You'll Find Me Now,' I'm twenty-two again, sitting heartbroken in my room, trying to figure out how to convince your mother to give me just a little more time to get my shit together. Trying to figure out how to write a song with one—eight hundredth of the emotional rawness."

I set the record I was holding back in the bin. I brought my hand to my mouth and nibbled at my fingernails. His face looked impossibly sad and I felt this sudden urge to make it better, but I didn't know how. "I don't know what to say."

"You don't have to say anything. Except . . ."

"What?"

"Why don't you try again?"

"Try again?"

"To tell me why you love music."

I stared at the tops of my red Chucks. "Dude. I don't know."

"Try."

I glanced up at him. There was an uncomfortable pause. "I don't—" I started.

"Just try," he repeated.

"Okay," I said slowly. "This may sound weird, but there are certain songs, like really great songs—you don't just listen to them, you know? They make you feel like they're listening back. Like the person who wrote the song heard you. Music makes you feel less alone in that way. It's proof that someone out there has felt the exact same way you do and they've managed to capture it in this perfect blend of words and sound."

Julian was staring at me intensely.

"What?"

He looked away for a moment and shook his shoulders, like he was trying to shed himself of an emotion. Escape it and pack it away. I recognized the gesture because I sometimes did the same thing. As I watched him, I remembered what Debra had told me about him feeling things too intensely.

"Julian?" I said.

When he turned back to me, he gave me a playful smile. The seriousness was gone. He lightly punched my shoulder. "That's my girl" was all he said, but it felt like so much more.

I shrugged him off, a heat creeping up my cheeks. But deep inside, something like pride, like recognition, uncoiled inside of me. As weird as it is to say, I was maybe, sort of, starting to fall in love with my dad. And he was maybe, sort of, starting to fall in love with me.

Most people don't remember falling in love with their parents. It's something that happens in between bites of pureed carrots and late nights in rocking chairs. But with Julian, it was different. It felt like a choice that I got to make. A choice we were making together.

"This is a moment I'm going to want to remember forever," he said.

"Okay. That's enough, cheeseball. Hallmark called. They want their lines back."

He laughed and leaned in to nudge me with his shoulder.

"No. Seriously, Tal. This is a monumental occasion. Our first trip together to a record store."

"Right."

"The first of many, I hope."

"Sure," I said, which sounded cagier than I meant it to.

But that didn't seem to bother him. "And since I want to always remember it, we should pick out a song to attach to the memory."

"Okay," I said slowly. "What did you have in mind?"

"Haven't decided. Let's hunt for something. What do you think?"

I hunched over another bin of records and started flipping through them. When I turned around to see if Julian had come up with anything good, I saw that Willowy Records was suddenly brimming with people.

"So I think someone blew up our spot," I whispered, taking in the clusters of people who were all excitedly hovering in proximity to Julian.

Julian sighed and pulled his sunglasses from their resting place in the V of his T-shirt. He grabbed my hand and we pushed through the crowd. People held up their phones to take photos. He politely waved in the general direction of the crowd but kept walking.

"I thought you told the kid at the register that you were gonna sign records."

Julian didn't answer that. We were quickly walking down

the main drag. There were people staring at us, but Julian was ignoring them, so I followed suit. All of a sudden, he stopped walking. He pointed at a building across the street.

"There it is."

"What?"

"The diner I told you about. Where I met your mother."

"The first one?"

"Yes," he said with a sad smile. "The first one."

"So are you ever going to tell me the rest of the story?"

He sighed and kept staring at the building. "I don't know, Tal."

"You don't know what?"

He shook his head as if shaking himself out of a memory. He put his hand on the small of my back and steered me toward the diner on the corner of the street. "Let's go in here and have a milk shake. And I'll tell you the rest of what I know."

As Lena stared at the marquee lit up with his name, her breath caught in her throat. It had been almost three full years since she'd last seen Julian Oliver.

Her roommate Marcy wrinkled her pert nose. "I still can't believe you know Julian Oliver. You've been holding out on me, Lena Abdallat."

Lena brushed off Marcy's comment and kept staring at the marquee. Just seeing his name felt like seeing a phantom—one she thought she'd previously exorcised—and she wasn't sure she would be able to handle being in his physical presence. It would be like seeing a zombie. She shivered and pulled her jean jacket closer.

"Seriously. How could you keep a secret like that?" Marcy flipped her platinum-blond hair, cut in a series of choppy layers designed to make her already prominent cheekbones even more prominent.

Lena shrugged. She thought of all the projects she'd completed over the last two years—sculptures filled with longing and collages of regret. Ones that she'd shown repeatedly in workshop. Ones that Marcy had critiqued. *I did tell you*, Lena thought. *Over and over again.*

"Lennie?" Marcy prompted. Lena had moved to New

York and had become Lennie thanks to Marcy.

Lena owed many thanks to the universe for connecting her with Marcy Barrows of Long Island. Marcy was an acrylic painter who was the youngest daughter of one of Manhattan's most sought-after divorce lawyers. She'd grown up in the city and was as New York as Lena was not.

There was a long line in front of the venue. Young people dressed from head to toe in faded denim, plaid shirts, and clunky boots. Wild animal prints and flowing skirts. Lena and Marcy breezed past the line as Julian had told her to do. The two of them looked mildly out of place, Marcy in her designer wrap dress and chandelier earrings, Lena in her black tunic and black leggings, the uniform she had adopted since moving to the city. She was wearing the charm bracelet Julian had found at a thrift store in Oak Falls and given to her on New Year's. It was supposed to have been a promise of their future together, the future that came crashing down a few months later.

As Marcy and Lena shoved through the line, some people shouted at them. Lena ignored the shouts; Marcy fearlessly flashed them the finger. "Oh, fuck off," Marcy said to one guy with a nose piercing. When they reached the front of the line, a large man stood with his arms crossed.

"There's a line, you know."

"Yes," Lena said hesitantly. She no longer struggled with

English, but when someone was confrontational she went back to feeling like the nervous girl struggling to communicate with the customs officer when she'd first landed in America five years ago.

"So why aren't you in it?"

"Because we're on the list, dummy," Marcy said, peering over Lena's shoulder. "Julian Oliver put us on the list."

The man looked skeptical. "What's your name?"

"Marcy Barrows."

"Lena Abdallat," Lena interjected. "It should be there. My name." She knew she sounded confused, but that's because she *was* confused. Not necessarily about what was happening—but about how she was supposed to feel.

What would she say to him? Was it a mistake to have come? What would it be like to see him onstage singing those songs—those songs that she thought of as so personal—those songs that were almost certainly all about her—for the whole world to hear? Her posture stiffened as she watched the security guard check his list.

"Well, hell. Surprise, surprise. Here you are. Lena Abdallat and guest."

Marcy raised her hand playfully. "That would be me. Guest."

The security guard handed Lena and Marcy necklaces adorned with plastic badges that read in big block letters: BACKSTAGE PASS. As Lena slipped hers over her thin neck, the security guard eyed her warily. "Have fun," he said, but it sounded more like "good luck" to her ears.

Marcy grabbed Lena's hand and pulled her inside the venue. It was an old ballroom. It reeked of marijuana and sweat. The lights were turned down low and it was mostly empty since they hadn't started to let the general public in yet.

Marcy leaned into Lena. "Are you nervous? You seem nervous."

"No," Lena lied. "I'm only worried it'll be strange since I haven't seen him in a long time." Lena hadn't been particularly forthcoming to Marcy about her relationship with Julian Oliver. Even when a poster of Julian's face landed in Times Square, Lena had kept her past secret from Marcy. She certainly hadn't explained that she'd heard seven of the nine tracks on Julian's now-famous album, *Winter in Indiana*, before the album was released. That he'd played her those songs on his acoustic guitar while they snuggled in his tiny apartment as gray snow had slowly blanketed the frozen ground outside. That each and every one of those songs was about her.

Or at least she'd thought those songs had been about her. Were about her. She felt dizzy, standing in the foyer of the cavernous decaying ballroom. The sheer size of it shocked her. He was going to fill this room? And the current emptiness of it made her feel sick with nerves.

Outside it was only a slightly chilly spring day, but she was suddenly unbearably cold. She was about to turn on her heel, head back to her apartment, crawl under the sheets, and read a book (she'd recently been making her way through the Western canon and had developed a particular penchant for Jane Austen's novels—she was presently reading *Mansfield Park*), when she saw him.

He was standing on the stage looking out at her. He moved toward her and Marcy. In the shadows of the hollowed-out room, it was hard to read his face. He hopped off the stage and continued to walk toward her. His pace became quicker the closer he got to her. She held her breath, almost convinced he was going to run past her.

But then, before she could really process what was happening, he'd lifted her off the floor. He twirled her and then set her back on her feet. "You came!" he said, the joy in his voice palpable. "You really came!"

She swallowed and simply nodded because she didn't trust her own voice.

"And look at you," he said, his eyes hungrily taking in her all-black ensemble. "You look so New York."

"That's taken a bit of work," Marcy said, stepping out in front of Lena and extending her hand in Julian's direction. "I'm Marcy Barrows. I believe we have a mutual friend."

That was so like Marcy. Lena loved her dearly and was grateful to her for all her help, but sometimes, Lena felt like

Marcy viewed her as a project—her "immigrant friend." Sometimes their relationship was a little too White Man's Burden for Lena's liking, but she knew Marcy meant well.

"It seems we do," Julian said jovially. He shook Marcy's hand, but never took his eyes off Lena. His cool blue eyes searched hers. They had more gray in them than she remembered. And they were asking her thousands of questions. Like, *How have you been? And did you miss me? And do you regret smashing everything we had together and leaving it behind?*

Lena knew she should say something. Anything. But her mind was buzzing, and it was difficult enough to think, let alone in English. Millions of Arabic phrases fired through her brain, and when she was able to distill her emotions down to one isolated kernel, she realized it was: longing.

She'd missed him.

Desperately.

And when she let her heart acknowledge that, it ached under the weight of everything else she was missing. Namely, home. Namely, her mother. God, she wanted her mother. She wanted to be home. She wanted to be home so, so badly.

She blinked back the tears that she felt forming in her eyes, and Julian reached out and grasped her hands. Even though she'd always taken such pains to hide her homesickness from him, he had a sixth sense for when a bout was coming on. And even though it had been months and months since he'd had the chance to comfort her, he was still able to steady her with his reassuring touch.

He watched her eyes soften as she regained composure. "So how have you been, Lena Abdallat?" he asked. "It's been a New York minute."

She swallowed again. "Isn't the better question how have you been?" She gestured toward the stage. "It's all coming true for you."

He bowed his head a little bit. "I told you it would. Patience."

She tensed and pulled her hands away from him. Such a simple word: patience. But it felt like an indictment. A reminder that she hadn't been patient. That she hadn't waited on him to get his shit together.

Truly, though, when she'd left Oak Falls, she'd had absolutely zero faith that Julian would get his shit together. It was her turn to give him a searching look. She wondered when he'd told his father he was dedicating everything toward becoming a musician. That his plan was to leave Oak Falls, to live a life that was radically different from Mr. Oliver's.

Julian had once told her he couldn't abandon his family business because his father had threatened that if Julian didn't take over the store, he would simply shutter it. She'd known Julian was terrified of creating more emotional distance between himself and his father.

Maybe it had gone down like how he'd crooned on "Finally, Always," the closing track on *Winter in Indiana*. She'd taken that track to be a personal admonition to her. But in the song, he'd sung, "Told you to be patient/But you said you had to go/You were right about your reasons/But now I've owned my own/So will you come back and be patient now?" and her heart had shattered when she first heard the song.

She'd thought: *Yes. Finally, always.*

And then when he'd called she could hardly believe it.

"I'm coming to New York," he'd said.

"Julian," she'd said.

"Please, Lena. I don't want to have this conversation over the phone. That's why I'm calling."

She'd smiled and twisted her hand around the phone's cord. "You're calling me on the phone to tell me that you don't want to talk on the phone?"

"You're still you," he'd said, and she'd heard relief in his voice. It was almost as though he'd been genuinely afraid that in the past two years she'd morphed into an entirely different person. But that was one of the main differences between her and him—the difference that had proved to be too insurmountable to overcome when push came to shove. She didn't believe that people could really change. And he did. He believed in anything if it was given time.

"More or less," she'd said.

"I want to see you."

"When you're in New York?"

"I was thinking that was my best shot. I didn't think you'd

agree to my offer to fly you out to come meet me right now in San Francisco."

She'd held her breath like she was considering this even though she really wasn't. "New York would be better."

"I thought so."

"Will you go to dinner with me?"

She held her breath again. "I want to hear you play."

"You've already heard me play."

"I want to hear you play these songs."

"You've already heard me play these songs." There was an edge to his voice.

"Not all of them. Not 'Finally, Always.' I love that song."

There was silence on the other end of the phone.

"You like that one, huh?" he finally said.

She wound the cord tighter around her fingers. "Yeah."

She wanted to say: *Did you write it for me? Do you forgive me for being impatient? For leaving you behind in Indiana? I'm so proud of you, Julian.*

And even though she didn't say any of those things, he still said, "You know that song was for you, right?"

"I thought so." Her voice had turned tiny and timid. Julian used to refer to it as her mouse voice.

"So will you see me?"

She didn't want to agree to dinner just yet. She didn't even know if she could handle it, if her heart could handle it. She didn't trust herself to sit calmly across the table from him. How could she be expected to share a bread basket with him, smile, and pretend like they hadn't smashed each other to smithereens?

"Julian" was all she said.

"That doesn't sound good."

"We destroyed each other. Do you really want to visit the wreckage?" She remembered the long fights in Oak Falls where she'd accused him of being a lazy coward and he'd accused her of being impatient and impractical and of having standards that were too damn high.

Of course I do, she'd thought when he'd accused her of that. *I want more of you. I want more for you. I want more of everything. No one puts an ocean between themselves and their home who isn't wildly, madly in search of more.*

There was a long pause on the phone. She wondered where he was calling from. Maybe San Francisco. He'd mentioned San Francisco. She imagined him at a pay phone on a hilly street, but then quickly corrected that mental image. Did successful musicians use pay phones? He was probably calling her from some fancy hotel room with a fluffy bed adorned with five-hundred-thread-count sheets. There was probably some model next to him right now, her silky blond hair spilling over the neighboring pillow. The thought made Lena's stomach coil, though she knew she had no right to be jealous. She'd given up that right when she left him standing heartbroken on the back porch of his family's home, his whole face begging her not to go, his blue eyes ringed with red.

When Julian hadn't said anything for a whole minute, she pressed the phone's receiver closer to her ear. She heard his shallow breathing and was filled with relief that he hadn't hung up, but then chastised herself for caring.

"Yes," he said. "I do. I do want to visit the wreckage, Lena. I want to rebuild everything. With you."

The relief she'd felt moments before was amplified. And a fluttery feeling of hope bubbled in her stomach and got stronger as she replayed in her head what he'd just said.

Despite knowing better, despite knowing so much better, she said, "Fine. I'll come to your show. Are tickets still available?"

He laughed, and the sound of his laugh amplified her hopeful excitement. "Don't be silly. I'll put you on the list. When you get to the venue, just walk past the line to the guy at the front. Tell him your name and he'll let you in."

"Okay." Her head was reeling. She couldn't believe this was his world now. Lists. Nondescript security guards. Doling out free tickets like candy.

"And Lena?"

"Yeah?"

"Try to get there early so I can see you before the show."

"Okay," she said again.

"Okay then. I'll see you in April."

She heard the phone click, him hanging up, but she didn't put the receiver back in its place. She held on to it, handling it with care as though it were a fragile object, as though it were a bomb.

"Lena?" Julian said, bringing her back to the present. "I was only teasing about the patience because . . ." He hung his head and slid his hands into the pockets of his pants. "I didn't mean to upset you."

"I know," she said, her eyes greedily taking him in. He was dressed in a green flannel shirt and tight black jeans. A variation of the outfit she'd seen him wearing in the various profiles of him that had been printed in various newspapers. "The Grunge God," the newspapers had declared him. One publication had gone so far as to deem him "The Prince of Melancholy." She'd rolled her eyes at this and imagined— hoped—he found those monikers laughable too. Though she'd, of course, clipped out all of the articles and saved them in an unassuming manila folder.

For posterity, she'd told herself. *Only to remember.*

After all, she was an immigrant. She was practiced in the art of remembering—in false memories and nostalgia. In the magic of keeping the past alive.

"Of course you do," he said, and his lips spread into an easy grin. His eyes shot around the ballroom, and she found herself wishing he'd focus on her. In the entirety of their relationship, she'd never struggled to get his attention, let alone hold it. "So what do you think of this place?"

An unexpected feeling of discomfort and disorientation overcame her. "It's fine, I guess."

"Fine? Man, I know you're hard to impress, but Jesus." He ran his hand through his hair. It was blonder than she remembered. Maybe they had him dye it. Something about that thought made her irritated.

She shrugged and stared down at her shoes. They were the nicest pair she owned, but in the dusty light of the ballroom she could see all of their scratches and discoloring. They felt insufficient. She felt insufficient.

"I shouldn't have come. I'm sorry, Julian. I thought I could do this, but I can't." She turned on her heel and darted toward the exit.

He followed behind her. He touched her arm gently. "Lena. Wait."

"Um." Marcy cleared her throat. "I don't mean to be awkward, but . . . do you guys have some kind of history that I don't know about?"

Julian and Lena stared at each other for a moment. They'd both forgotten Marcy was even there. That she'd been standing beside them the whole time. They started to laugh, high-pitched and uneasy.

"I'll take that as a yes," Marcy said. She whistled and tossed her hair back. "Is there a bar in here?"

Julian laughed some more, the nerves giving way to

a more easygoing and joyful sound. "Yeah. I don't know if they're open yet, but Mikey can take care of you." As if he'd simply been hiding in the shadows, waiting to be summoned—which, sadly, he probably had—Mikey appeared beside Julian.

"Yeah, boss?"

"Boss?" Lena said, her mouth gaping slightly. She clasped her hands together with excitement. Mikey gave her a blank stare. "Mikey! It's me."

Mikey looked confused for a moment and then the wave of recognition hit him. "Lena! Of course! Julian said we'd be seeing you in New York."

She briefly felt wounded by that statement. She knew she shouldn't have been, but it made her feel like just one of the various women Julian had arranged to see on this tour. Melissa in New Orleans, Tabitha in Denver, and Lena in New York.

Mikey opened his arms and pulled her into a big bear hug. Though she knew it was just her nostalgic mind playing tricks on her, she swore she could still smell the cheeseburger grease on him, the faint sweetness of a vanilla milk shake. When she pulled away from the hug and studied him, she found him to be untouched by time. He still wore his brown hair shaggy, his skin was still lightly pockmarked, and he still had the hunched-forward posture of someone who was always reaching for something.

"It's good to see you, Lena," Mikey said, and he sounded like he really meant it.

"Boss?" she said, repeating the phrase she'd heard Mikey use earlier.

Mikey's face flushed red. He seemed both pleased and embarrassed. "A joke," Mikey said. "You know, since I was his boss back in the day at the diner and now he's, well you know, he's *Julian Oliver*."

Lena turned her attention to Julian. "He's always been Julian Oliver."

Julian took her hand and gave it an unexpected squeeze. Her whole body hummed with the satisfaction of recognition. *I'm doomed*, she thought, and returned the squeeze.

"As heartwarming as this reunion is, could I get that drink?" Marcy declared with another one of her signature whistles.

"Sure thing, baby doll," Mikey said. "Believe me, I know, these two are insufferable as hell." He winked at Lena, and she felt like she'd jumped back in time, as though she were sitting at one of the metal tables at Mickey's, waiting for Julian to bring her out a sloppily made vanilla milk shake that was thoroughly mediocre but somehow still managed to taste like the best thing in the world.

Mikey led Marcy away from the main hollowed-out room, presumably to fix her a drink. Lena felt the absence of their presence, the weight of finally, after all this time, being alone with Julian.

"Mikey is going to like your friend."

"Her name is Marcy," Lena said sharply.

Julian smiled good-naturedly. "Of course. Marcy."

"I'm sure you've noticed she's very pretty." She hated how jealous she sounded.

Julian's smile stayed on his face. He didn't say anything.

The thing was, Marcy was pretty. And rich. And interesting. And now that Julian was, well, Julian Oliver, it seemed like, on paper, he should, would, be a much better fit with Marcy Barrows.

"Lena," Julian said.

"Yes?"

He grabbed for her hand again. She didn't pull away from his touch. "Since you walked into this room, the only person I saw was you." He dropped her hand, but she could still feel his skin lingering on hers.

He ran his hand through his hair. It had gotten longer since she'd seen him last. *Musician hair*, she thought. *Rock star hair*. "Hell, I think since the moment I met you, you've been the only person I've been able to see. At the very least, you're certainly the only person I've wanted to see." He let out a loud exhale. It was the sound of someone who had been holding his breath for a very long time. "I wrote this whole album for you." Then he added, "I'm doing all of this for you."

She surprised herself when she said, "I know."

His smile was back and it'd crept into his eyes. "Of course you do."

She heard the click of Marcy's heels. She and Mikey were heading back toward them.

"We don't have much time before they start letting everyone in," Julian said.

"Everyone?" Lena wiggled her eyebrows in a way that she hoped was flirtatious. She'd never been talented at flirting. She'd come to learn that America was a very flirtatious culture, a land of innuendo and winks. Before, she'd never had to flirt with Julian. There had been no reason to. She'd had his attention and his love. She could be true with him, no pretense. No acting.

Mikey and Marcy stood off to the side. Marcy was swaying back and forth slightly, triumphantly clutching what appeared to be a gin and tonic. She took a refined sip. "Can we join you guys, or do you need more time to hash out this history I had no idea you had?"

Lena tried to swallow her annoyance at Marcy. She wished she would get a clue and just give her and Julian some space.

Marcy turned her shoulders to face Julian. "Can you believe what a hold-out Lena is? She only told me that she knew you."

Julian didn't take his eyes off Lena. She felt like a brat, but satisfaction bubbled in her stomach. "She does know me."

"Yeah. But." Marcy took another sip of her gin and tonic. "You know what I mean."

"Julian," Mikey interjected. "The show's starting."

Julian still didn't take his eyes off Lena. Lena kept looking from him to Marcy to Mikey to the vacant stage and then back to him, and she always found his eyes locked on her. She held her breath.

"It'll be different this time," he said.

Her nerve was slipping a bit because of the presence of Marcy and Mikey, but she straightened her spine and demurred, "How do you know there will even be a this time?"

"Because I'm patient. And persistent." He walked toward her, brushed her hair away from her face, and kissed her gently on the cheek. "Enjoy the show. I'll see you after, okay?"

Once he and Mikey were gone, Lena found herself alone with Marcy, staring at the vacant stage.

"What the fuck, Len?" Marcy said. "You used to date Julian Oliver? You didn't think to mention that?"

Lena looked down at her shoes, which had seemed so ratty moments ago. They didn't seem so bad anymore. "I told you that I knew him."

Marcy nudged her shoulder against Lena. "I always knew you were a badass chick, but damn."

Lena wanted to smile, but she felt unworthy of the

compliment. That's another thing she'd decided about Americans. The only thing they loved more than being praised themselves was praising others. Oftentimes when it was inappropriate to do so. Nothing was cheaper in America than compliments. "He wasn't a rock star then."

She turned her head at the sound of the doors swinging open. Suddenly and without warning, the room began to fill with eager bodies. All of them buzzing with anticipation, all of them desperate to catch a glimpse of Julian Oliver.

The show started, and Lena tuned out for most of the opening act. It wasn't that they weren't good, but her mind wasn't in a place where it was able to focus. The only thing she managed to note about the band was that they had a female bassist, and she was very pretty, and Lena pettily wondered if Julian had a) noticed how pretty the bassist was and b) if they'd ever had a thing. She found herself comparing her own looks to the bassist's.

She looked back down at her shoes. They seemed scratched and worn again.

By the time Julian came on, she was knotted with worry and jealousy. Her head was foggy with confusion. But this show was so different from the one in Oak Falls. The music was on pace. The band composed. And when Julian started to play his songs, she felt the music drape over her like a blanket. Those songs were like lullabies.

So it shouldn't have come as a surprise to anyone,

especially herself, that three hours later she found herself in a chic candlelit restaurant, sitting across from Julian, nervously sipping her second glass of champagne.

"So how'd this all happen?" she asked.

"What?"

"You know what I mean. You went from zero to sixty."

"You leaving was the kick in the ass I needed," Julian said.

And this declaration made Lena both unbearably happy and unbearably sad. She took another gulp of champagne.

Julian explained to her that once she'd left, he, Marty St. Clair, and Chris had kicked the band into overdrive. They'd fired their previous drummer and found a new, much more talented guy. Every moment that Julian wasn't working in his father's store, he was writing new songs and practicing with the band. About a year after Lena left, they all drove out to a band showcase in Chicago.

Marty was pushy and charismatic enough to get them some face time with a record label rep. The rep clearly wasn't expecting much and gave them the chance to play one song. Julian convinced the group to go with "Finally, Always," and the rep ended up flipping for it. He signed them to the label with a small advance.

No one predicted the record would take off in the way that it did. But then two amazing things happened: 1) a much bigger, more established band had issues in the recording studio, which freed up some marketing money and b) a music critic at *Rolling Stone* fell head over heels for S.I.T.A.'s album when he was sent an advance copy to listen to. Before Julian knew it, the band was playing sold-out shows, and each venue seemed bigger than the last.

"What do your parents think?" Lena asked. "They must be so excited."

Julian stared down at the table. "You know how they are. Mom is thrilled. Dad is . . ."

Lena reached across the table for his hand. "I'm sure he's proud of you."

Julian sighed and looked up. "I think he just thought I'd finally grown up, you know? I was working at the store. I was doing well. And then one day, I just didn't show up." He shook his head. "I took the cowardly way out. I told them over the phone."

"I'm sure they understand."

"Dad's store is in trouble. It isn't turning a profit anymore. I sent them a check in the mail, but Dad refused to accept it." He continued to shake his head. "It's like he blames me for the store closing. But it's not my fault, is it?"

Lena reached across the table and squeezed his hand. "It's definitely not your fault. He'll come around."

"We don't really talk anymore. It's even worse than it was before," Julian said. "I'm worried there's a distance growing between us that's soon going to be insurmountable.

He just makes it so difficult to talk."

"It'll be okay," Lena assured him, even though she wasn't quite sure that it would be.

That dinner easily gave way to her spending the night in his hotel room. The next morning, Julian held her tightly on the busy sidewalk outside the hotel.

"Don't go," he pleaded.

"I have to graduate," Lena insisted. "But then I promise I'll come join you on tour."

He kissed her forehead. "Maybe I should just stay here."

"Don't be silly."

"I don't want to let you go again."

"It's different this time," she said.

"You promise?"

"I promise."

"You promise?" he repeated.

And she laughed as he smothered her with kisses.

Lena finished up school and, as promised, joined Julian for the summer leg of his tour. She was working on finishing a collection of human-sized clay figurines and was thrilled when she discovered a gallery—not the most elite, but a prominent one nonetheless—was interested in displaying them. She was sure that Julian, or someone he knew now, had been responsible for the gallery's interest, but she tried not to think about that too much.

Be proud, she implored herself. *Your dreams are coming true.*

She was so focused on making her own dreams come true that it was beginning to cause friction between her and Julian. It wasn't something that happened overnight, but slowly their relationship began to erode. Julian was always inviting her to go out with him after the show to various parties where he was expected to make an appearance.

Lena hated those parties.

Sure, one reason was that she didn't like being treated like she was only interesting because she was Julian Oliver's girlfriend. She was a person with thoughts and dreams and interests completely separate from him. Also, she simply preferred to stay at home so she could work on her own art.

Julian's newfound fame hadn't made her lazy. In fact it was the opposite—it had made her even wilder with ambition. She was determined to catch up with him. The way she saw it, they had stood on the same starting line, and he had somehow managed to get many strides ahead, and so now it was her job to close the gap.

Julian did not see it this way.

"Why are you so worried, babe?" he would ask, wrapping his arms around her waist and pulling her close. He would shower her neck with kisses and beg her to come relax with him instead of repainting the face on one of the clay figurines for the umpteenth time. "You shouldn't worry so much. Everything's going to fall into place for us.

Hell, it's fallen into place for us."

"You mean," Lena corrected, "it's fallen into place for you."

Julian did not understand this distinction that Lena drew between the Us—their relationship—and their singular artistic pursuits. He saw them as one unit. As a team. He couldn't process why Lena wanted to untangle herself from that unit.

But Lena deeply believed that something wasn't yours unless you, and only you, earned it. Only you owned it. Sharing Julian's success did not interest her. She wanted her own success. Something that had her own name on it. She was unapologetic in this desire, and it began to drive Julian crazy.

He stayed out later and later at the parties she refused to attend with him. She knew those parties were full of girls. Girls that fawned all over him, girls that she desperately wanted to believe he wasn't sleeping with. He came home smelling of smoke and alcohol. His words blurred and his hands clumsy. When she would question him, he would fire back at her.

"Why isn't this enough for you?" he asked her one night, his voice hoarse, his eyes far away. "I wrote the album, I left home, I did all of this for you."

"Because it's not mine," she said quietly. She wished there was some way she could explain to him that she hadn't put a whole ocean between herself and her home to be a rock star's sidekick. It wasn't enough. It wouldn't ever be enough.

"But I'm yours," he said sadly.

"I know," she whispered. "But that's not enough."

"I wish it was," he said, and she knew he wasn't only thinking of her. He was thinking of his father.

Things continued to deteriorate between them. More fights. More late nights where Julian didn't show up until three a.m., and when he did show up he was drunk and reeking of cigarette smoke.

It was on one of those nights when she was holed up in another random hotel room, sitting on the floor with her sketch pad, doodling ideas for her next project, when the phone rang. She picked it up, bracing herself for Mikey's voice covering for Julian, who had inevitably gotten too wasted at one of the after-show parties.

It was her cousin.

"Lena?" her cousin said, her voice shaky.

"Yes?" Lena said brusquely, irritated to have been interrupted from her work.

"It's your mother."

Lena's heart stalled. She squeezed the phone and let out a tiny whimper of a prayer.

"She's gone," her cousin said softly.

Lena fell to her knees.

Her cousin continued to talk. Whispering words of

comfort. Filling in the details. Explaining that she and her husband didn't know if they would be able to go home for the funeral. But Lena surely would, wouldn't she? And then the cousin asked whether Julian would go with Lena.

A shivering dread snaked its way into her cloud of grief. Would Julian come with her? Did she even want him to? Would she even be able to go herself? Her student visa was about to expire. She didn't know if she'd be able to get back into the country. Plus, the money. She couldn't afford a ticket home without Julian's help.

She hung up the phone and sat for what seemed like hours paralyzed on the bed. She stared out at the nondescript room that could've been anywhere in the world and whispered to herself, "My mother is dead.

"My mother is dead," she repeated over and over again.

But no matter how many times she said it, it never clicked. It never seemed fully true. She kept waiting for the enormity of it to hit her, but it didn't. She kept feeling sharp pieces of sadness, but she was waiting for the final stab to come down.

She didn't understand how something so momentous could happen so quickly. She had always childishly believed that you would be prepared for the death of your parent. At least it had been that way with her father. He had been sick. They had all waited and watched him die. It hadn't made it easier, but she had known it was coming.

The shock of this grief was what she couldn't process. Her

mother's heart had simply given out. Lena placed her hand over her own heart. She wondered how many more beats it had in store for her.

It wasn't that night that she left for good. She stayed on tour with the band for at least another month. At first, Julian even harbored some hope that the death of Lena's mother was going to bring them closer together. Lena started coming out to more of the after-parties. Her desire to not be alone seemed to be the strongest effect of her grief.

But then one afternoon, completely unexpectedly, Lena marched into their hotel room and said, "I'm leaving." And then added, "For good."

"What?" Julian had said. He was waking up from an afternoon nap in the hotel bed. His eyes were still groggy with sleep.

She sat on the love seat in the corner. When he sat up in bed and really looked at her, he saw that she was different. He didn't know how. But she was. She felt so far away even though he could've reached out and touched her. Later, he would think it had been like looking at a hologram version of a person.

"I'm going back to school to become a doctor. I know I won't be earning a degree as a medical doctor, but it will still be a doctorate. It will still be something instead of nothing," she said flatly. "My mother is dead and I betrayed her while she was alive by lying to her about my new life in the States.

But now, I'm going to make things right. I'm going to make things right for her memory."

Julian shook his head. "Lena, isn't this what you always lectured me about? You have to live your life for you. You can't apologize or feel guilty for having your own dreams. Your mother would be so proud of you. I know she would."

Lena tilted her head down to stare at the hotel carpet. It was cream-colored and plush. "That's a luxury only afforded to you, Oliver," she said, and stood up from the love seat. "I've already told Mikey I'm leaving. He's booked my flight for this afternoon."

"Lena," he said, jumping out of the bed. "Wait. Please."

But she didn't wait. She left.

And she never came back.

III.

gaped at Julian. We were sitting in the very back booth of the small diner he'd steered me into.

When we'd come in, he'd introduced me to the man who'd greeted us at the door.

"This is Joe, my manager Mikey's little brother," he said. And then once we'd taken a seat at the booth he'd added, "Good people. The whole family."

An untouched plate of French fries sat in front of us. And two similarly untouched vanilla milk shakes. The whipped cream had begun to melt, and the maraschino cherry was dangerously close to nose-diving into the ice cream.

"She just left?"

Julian shrugged and stretched out his hands, drumming his fingers against the table. I stared at the fries, which were starting to look particularly greasy under the fluorescent lights of the diner.

"Yeah, kid. She just left."

"But that doesn't make any sense."

"Tell me about it."

I gave him a you-know-what-I-mean glare. "Didn't you call her?"

"I called her over and over again. I flew to try and visit her. She rebuffed me, Taliah. She wanted nothing to do with me."

"And you just gave up?"

He hung his head. "I had to respect what she wanted. I didn't let go, but I let her let go. That's all there was left to do."

A rosy-tinted love song came on over the diner's speakers. Julian flinched a little.

"Not your jam?" I asked.

"Not particularly," he admitted, smiling sheepishly.

"Was your way of not letting go to write songs about Mom?"

He nodded. "That's kind of my brand, isn't it? A certain type of unrequited melancholy." He tapped his fingers on the tabletop. "You know the pause in 'That Night'?"

I nodded. Of course I did. It was one of S.I.T.A.'s biggest hits, if not their most famous song, and was well known for a part where the music cuts out completely. You think the song is over, and then all of a sudden, the music starts again at full blast. It takes the listener by surprise, and the first time you hear it, you're truly thrilled to realize the song isn't actually over yet.

"That pause was always sort of a metaphor for my inability to let go." He shrugged in a way that made him seem younger. Helpless, almost. "I've never been good at endings."

My insides swelled with several different conflicting emotions. I couldn't believe that Mom in some ways was directly responsible for one of the most famous stylistic choices in a modern rock song. That was pretty freaking cool. But it was also devastatingly sad. As I looked at Julian, I could see that even after all these years, he still wasn't sure how to let it go.

"I think most of your songs end in a pretty satisfactory way," I offered.

He gave me a little nod.

I thought about it some more. "I still don't understand why she just left. Why then?" I narrowed my eyes. "Are you sure you're telling me everything?"

Julian fidgeted. Something crossed his face, but it was gone quickly.

"What?" I said.

Julian kept folding and unfolding his sunglasses. Putting

them on the edge of the table and picking them back up.

"What is it?" I pressed.

He let out a deep sigh. "I mean, your mom and I weren't in the best place then."

"What does that mean?"

"You know," he hedged.

"No. I don't. That's why I'm asking."

He tilted his head back and ran his hand through his hair. "I don't know, Taliah. We were fighting a lot. She thought I was partying too much. She thought I was cheating on her." He held up his hands. "Which I wasn't. I maybe was too flirtatious with fans at times, but I never cheated on her."

"Okay," I said slowly, unsure that I fully believed him.

"And I thought she resented my success. So you see, we fought over normal, petty things and suspicions. I just didn't realize how bad it had gotten until it was over."

I wasn't sure what he was describing fell firmly into the category of normal, given that most people weren't famous musicians, but I understood what he was trying to say. "You think her mother's death just changed her?"

He slumped down in a defeatist way. "I think that was probably the catalyst for it. But she gave up on me, on us. She left."

I felt like I should defend Mom, but I didn't know how to. A knot formed in my throat. "Do you think she knew about me? You know, she always told me that my father was

someone from back home in Jordan. She says they recon-
nected during her mother's funeral, and she didn't realize
she was pregnant until she was back in the States."

Julian pinched his lips together. "I don't know if she knew
she was pregnant at the time she left, but I've been wondering that too. And I can't decide if that makes it better or
worse."

I nodded a little. "It just doesn't seem like Mom. She's
never struck me as a rash person."

Julian made a noncommittal sound.

"Okay, okay. But you know what I mean," I offered. I
reached out for my milk shake. I gripped the sides of the cold
glass and spun it around.

"Yeah," he said. "Something doesn't add up. But sometimes I wonder if I think something is off because I want it to
be. Instead of the cold hard truth—that she just didn't want
me anymore. That she was done waiting for me to turn into
a person who didn't disappoint her."

I leaned forward in the booth. There was something I
wanted to say but was afraid to. "For what it's worth," I said
slowly, "you haven't been a disappointment to me."

Julian's face slowly broke into a smile. A small one. But a
smile nonetheless. "Really?"

"Yeah. Really."

"That's something, Tal. That's really something." The
vulnerability and rawness of his voice reminded me of the

way he sang some of S.I.T.A.'s most popular songs. It also made me want to cry. Julian's hand instinctively went to his eyes. I could tell he was a little embarrassed that he was getting so emotional. He put his sunglasses back on and crossed his arms, slouching back down in the booth.

I chewed on my lower lip. "I'm sorry."

He jerked to look at me. "Sorry? What for?"

I shrugged and sank into the booth. "For being difficult. For being sort of distant. It's just hard for me . . . it's always just been me and Mom, you know? I'm trying to figure out how this—you, this other piece—fits."

"I get that." He gave me a sad smile. "Is that why you don't want to talk to me about your own music?"

I stared down at the booth's tabletop. "Not exactly."

"Taliah, what is it?"

"It's just," I said, squirming in my seat, "I feel dumb. You're like a rock star. And I'm this wannabe. I don't want to be some second-rate carbon copy of you."

"Look," he said, and he reached across the table. "You never have to worry about being some second-rate carbon copy of me."

I blushed. "You don't know that. You've only heard one of my songs. The rest of them could all be like the musical equivalent of bad fan fiction of your albums."

He laughed. "I doubt that." And then paused. "Wait. Are they?"

"No," I said, shaking my head and laughing a little. "Maybe someday I'll play the rest of them for you."

His whole face broke into a grin. "I'd love that."

"Not yet, though," I said quickly.

"I know," he said. "I'm willing to wait. We have time."

Something washed over his face. Sadness maybe. Longing.

"Are you thinking about your dad?" I asked softly.

He nodded. "I think the thing that hurts the most right now is I'm grieving all the moments I lost. All the times I didn't call home or visit. All the times I didn't just sit him down and force him to talk about our issues with me." He sighed. "I wish I was spending more time feeling nostalgic for the memories I do have, and less time feeling greedy and bitter about the memories I don't."

Before I could say anything in response, his phone started to ring. "Hello?" he answered.

His face fell. He nodded to himself and tersely said, "Okay. We'll be there."

Once he'd hung up, he turned to me. "We need to go to the hospital."

IV.

Debra and Sarah were already at the hospital when we arrived. And so were Carter and Brady. Everyone was huddled right outside Tom's room.

On the car ride over, Julian had explained that the doctors had told Debra that Tom's vitals were dropping. The time had come.

Debra embraced both of us, and Sarah pulled me into a tight hug. When she hugged me, I could feel how tense her body was; her grief was palpable.

"The boys and I have already been inside to see him. You should go," Sarah said.

I looked at Julian. I understood if he wanted to have this moment to himself, but he grabbed my hand and we entered Tom's hospital room. The room didn't look any different than yesterday, but it felt different. Maybe because we'd been told that this was the end, or maybe somehow the room knew it too.

Julian and I both walked up to the side of Tom's bed. Julian bowed his head and grabbed for his dad's hand.

"Are you sure you don't want a moment alone?" I asked.

Julian's jaw trembled. I could tell he was doing his best to choke back his emotion. "Maybe you could say your good-bye, and then I'll take a few moments?" he said.

I nodded. I stared at Tom. His eyes were closed and his body was still. If it weren't for the beeping monitor, I wouldn't have known he was still alive. I shivered slightly and wrapped my arms around myself.

It didn't feel right that I was there. As I looked down at his motionless face, I became overwhelmed with questions. But I knew they were the wrong ones. I wanted to know if he'd seen this moment coming. If he was prepared for it. And if he was scared. I wanted to know if he would've done things differently.

This was the closest I'd ever been to someone who was about to die, and I couldn't stop wondering what was going on inside his mind.

Julian squeezed Tom's hand and let out a slow exhale. I

knew he was waiting for me to say something. Anything.

So I awkwardly said, "I'm really glad I got the opportunity to meet you. And that you think I have my mother's nose." Then I winced, unsure if I'd crossed some line, but Julian made a sound of amusement and smiled a little. "Debra yesterday told me you were a secret fan of S.I.T.A. I wish we'd gotten a chance to talk about records. I would've loved to know what your favorite album is." I felt a pressure building in my throat.

I suddenly felt mortified, like I had said the wrong thing. But then Julian walked over to me and hugged me.

Really hugged me. In a way he hadn't ever before. He rested his chin against the top of my head and whispered, "Thank you."

When he released me from the hug, I could see that his eyes were filling with tears. He self-consciously patted at his eyes. "I'll meet up with you outside. Okay, kid?"

I gave him a slight nod, and on my way out, I caught sight of him kneeling beside Tom's bed. There was something about his posture that told me he was learning how to say good-bye. How to let go.

V.

We left Debra alone at the hospital. That had been her request. It was implicitly understood that Tom would pass within the next few hours. Julian and I rode in silence for the first part of the drive back to the Oliver farmhouse.

There was something different about him. I couldn't quite put my finger on it. Sure, he was grieving. But he also seemed more comfortable. Less antsy. His leg wasn't constantly bouncing, he wasn't tapping his fingers against the steering wheel.

"He said something to me," Julian said.

I turned my head to look at him. "What?"

"Yeah," Julian said, almost as though he couldn't believe it himself. "It was faint, but I swear I heard it."

He was staring straight ahead and he looked almost lost in the memory. "He said, *Fireproof*."

"The title of your third album?"

Julian nodded. He still looked deep in thought. "My most unpopular album." He let out a sound that sort of resembled a laugh. "But I think my dad was trying to tell me it was his favorite album." He glanced over at me quickly. His face was full of unbridled surprise. "I think my dad was trying to tell me he liked my music."

We came to a red light and Julian rested his weight against the steering wheel of the car. "Holy shit, right?"

"Yeah," I said weakly because I didn't know what else to say.

"And it's all thanks to you, Tal."

"Huh?"

"You're the one who brought it up. You asked him what his favorite album was. I think he was answering you."

I shook my head. "No. I don't think so . . . I . . ."

"Taliah," he said firmly. "I know so. And thank you."

I stared down at my sneakers, feeling very unworthy of the compliment. "You should thank your mom. She's the one

245

who told me Tom liked your music."

Julian whistled lightly. "I know it seems like such a small thing, but that brought me so much closure. I think my dad maybe respected what I've dedicated my life to. Maybe he didn't always understand it, but I think he was letting me know that he respected it. That means everything, you know?"

"Yeah," I said. "He accepted that version of yourself."

"Exactly," Julian said. "You know, a couple of hours ago I thought that once my dad died, my relationship with him would be over. And I thought it was so fucked up that the universe was going to let him die when I still hadn't worked things out with him. But I'm starting to think that's not the case. I still have the chance to work through things. My dad and I still have a relationship. It's just changed."

I was silent as I thought about that for a moment. I wondered if he was right. If relationships really have a life of their own, if they live on. I hoped he was.

He steered the car into the Olivers' long, gravelly driveway. "I don't think we're going to have a proper funeral for Dad."

"Oh?"

"No. Sarah's going to host a memorial. Mom says he wanted to be cremated. She's going to keep his ashes and eventually sprinkle them out here." He gestured toward the acres of farmland that spread out on either side of the drive-way.

All of a sudden, Julian slammed on the brakes. I looked over at him and his eyes were glued on something up ahead in the distance. I followed his gaze and then I saw her.

My mother.

VI.

"Get in the car, Taliah" was the first thing Mom said to me when she saw me. Julian tried to reason with her, but she refused to even look in his direction.

"Mom," I pleaded. "Please. At least let me get my stuff from inside the house." This had been a white lie, since of course I hadn't packed anything, but it did the trick. Mom reluctantly followed me inside to the guest room.

"I'm not leaving," I said as I closed the door.

Mom paced around the bedroom, looking as polished as ever. She was dressed in black linen pants and a pale rose-colored blouse. Her hair was swept up in a bun. The only physical traces of unease I could detect were bags under her eyes. I wondered briefly if she had taken extra care with her appearance since she knew she would be seeing Julian.

"I can't believe you," I said again. It was a phrase I'd been repeating since I stepped out of Julian's car.

"Taliah, HB," she said calmly. "I understand why you're upset, but you have to understand."

I shook my head and sat down on the bed. "You don't get to tell me that I have to understand. You kept my father a secret, and me a secret from him. You lied to me about who he was, and even when I gave you a chance a few years ago to revise your story, you dug your heels into your lie."

"Tal," she said, and this time her voice was sharper. "Considering you ran away from home—"

"I didn't run away from home! I left with my own father. To come visit my dying grandfather."

She gave me a stern look. "Without my permission. When I was on the other side of the Atlantic Ocean and assumed you were at home. Do you understand how frightened I was when I heard your voicemail? I booked the first flight to Indianapolis I could and raced here. I was so worried about you, Taliah. So, so worried."

I grabbed a pillow and pressed it against my chest. "Are you kidding me? You really want to lecture me about my poor choices when you're the one who lied to me my entire life? My entire freaking life, Mom." I hugged the pillow tightly. "You're the reason I never had the chance to meet Tom before his stroke. The reason my dad is—"

"I know," Mom said, cutting me off. She walked over to sit down beside me. "It's complicated, Taliah. Looking back, it felt like the right choice at the time. I know now that maybe it wasn't, but you have to understand that I was only trying to do what was best."

I looked down and saw Mom's hands were trembling. Threads of both anger and sadness pulsed through me. "But I don't understand. Help me understand?"

Mom squeezed her hands together in an attempt to steady them. "It's complicated."

"You keep saying that," I insisted. "But from what Julian told me—"

She shook her head sharply. "He shouldn't have told you anything."

My anger swallowed my sadness. "Why not? Don't you think I have the right to know?"

"Of course. But . . . I would've liked the opportunity to be the one to tell you."

"You had sixteen years."

"I know," she said softly. She didn't meet my gaze.

"Sixteen years," I repeated.

She finally looked up at me. She reached over and brushed a strand of hair away from my face. "I know, HB. I know. But I made a mistake. Can't you understand that?"

A mistake. It felt like more than a mistake. And I wanted to tell her that. It felt like a betrayal. But she looked so sad, and even though a large part of me wanted to cut into her some more, I held back. After everything that had happened today, I was tired of seeing people I cared about hurt.

"Maybe," I said. "But I think you owe me an explanation."

"I do," she agreed.

"So?"

She shook her head again. "Not now. Right now, we should focus on your grandfather."

I couldn't believe that after sixteen years, she still wanted to wait. But I knew my mother well enough to know that even if I pushed it, she wasn't going to crack. At least not right now. So I pushed for something else. "So we can stay?"

She touched my cheek. "Until the memorial."

DAY FOUR

*(In Which I Learn to Understand That Some
Histories Have Not Yet Happened)*

I.

Tom passed away at 11:17 p.m. Even though we had all been anticipating it, it still hit everyone pretty hard. I could tell that Debra and Julian were relieved to no longer exist in a state of anxious anticipation, but the devastating finality of it still shook them.

I still wasn't quite sure where I fit in. I kept thinking the universe would whisper into my ear and tell me exactly how I should behave, how I should feel. It seemed like something like this should change you. Make you wiser. Make you understand things better, have a new and sharper perspective.

But I still felt like me. And I felt as clueless as ever.

Of course I was sad. But I didn't feel like I was as sad as I should've been. And again, I felt sad for mostly all the wrong reasons, which made me feel guilty.

I think my feelings of discomfort were exacerbated by my mother. I had expected her to feel even more awkward than I did, but if she did, she didn't show it. She immediately jumped right in, shooing Debra and Sarah out of the kitchen so she could unload the dishwasher and do other random and routine household chores.

She said she wanted to give Debra and Sarah time to focus on planning the memorial. She volunteered to go with Sarah into town to buy groceries for the memorial, which I found to be beyond weird. When she came back and I confronted her about it, she said, "Taliah. I don't know what you want from me. You asked to stay, and we stayed. So I'm just trying to be polite and help the Olivers through this difficult time."

I felt chastised, and maybe rightly so.

But the weirdest thing was how she pretended like Julian didn't exist. In the morning when she was emptying out the dishwasher, he walked into the kitchen to pour himself a bowl of cereal and was surprised to find her standing there.

"Hey," he said, and I could tell he was self-conscious from the fact that he kept tapping his spoon against the rim of his bowl.

My mom barely said hello back and sped to finish unloading the dishwasher and then excused herself to the basement, where she was running a load of laundry.

Julian shot me a helpless look and I just gave him a shrug because I had no idea what to say.

It wasn't until much later that day that I overheard them talking. I walked out onto the back porch and heard my mother's voice. I looked around. She wasn't on the porch, but I knew it was her voice. And then I heard Julian's. I assumed that maybe they were standing out in the backyard, somewhere out of view of the porch.

"You're going to have to talk to me at some point," Julian said.

"Did you follow me out here?" Mom said, and I could tell from the sound of her voice that her arms were crossed. I knew that voice very well.

"Yes," he said, exasperated.

"Don't," she said. "Don't do this."

"Do what? Try to talk with you?"

"I know you're upset about Tom, but you can't use that as an excuse to . . ." Mom went silent.

"As an excuse to what, Lena? Ask you what happened to us?"

I heard my mom sigh. "What happened to us? You know what happened to us. It's the same thing that happens to everyone. We grew up. We changed."

"But I wanted to grow with you." Julian's voice made something inside me break. He sounded so desperate.

My mom didn't say anything. That somehow made it worse.

"And I should've had some say about Taliah," Julian said.

"Don't," my mom said sharply.

"Don't? You don't get to tell me that. I have the right to confront you about why you kept Taliah from me for all these years."

"All these years?" Mom's voice was full of defiance. "You don't get to rewrite history, Julian. You know as well as I do that you knew about Taliah long before you got her first letter."

My breath caught. I pressed my back against the wall of the porch and slid down to a sitting position.

"That's not fair, Lena," Julian said quietly.

"How is it not fair?" Mom's voice was as firm. "I called you when she was five."

Five? I pulled my knees to my chest, trying to ignore the panic that was coming over me.

"Exactly! Five! You robbed me of five years," Julian argued. "And then out of nowhere, you called me."

"And you robbed yourself of the other eleven," Mom seethed. "Don't you remember? You questioned me about whether she was really yours? That's when I knew I had made the right decision to keep you out of her life."

Julian didn't say anything.

"And then when you got her letter, you called me again," Mom continued, her voice icy. "But not because you wanted to meet her. Because you wanted to know what we *wanted* from you. And the answer to that is: nothing. I don't want anything from you, Julian."

I squeezed my eyes shut. I couldn't believe what I was hearing.

"You know that's not fair, Lena," Julian finally said. "When you first called me, I felt overwhelmed and confused. I hadn't heard from you in years, and you just sprang that on me. You have to cut me some slack."

"Oh," my mom hissed, "I'm sorry I didn't break the news to you in a more gentle manner."

"Stop," Julian pleaded. "I didn't understand."

"I think you did," Mom said.

"That's not fair," he repeated. "And not true." I could hear the anger in Julian's voice. I wished I knew whether he was angry because Mom was right or because she was wrong.

"I'm done fighting about this," Mom said. "What's done is done."

"I think that's exactly what we have to talk about. What was done. The decision you made!"

"Just let it go, Julian. I know I have." Mom sounded tired.

"Lena! Wait. I can't let it go," Julian said.

I crept around the porch, hoping to catch a glimpse of them. Out of the corner of my eye, I saw my mom heading toward me. She quickly adjusted the expression on her face to look normal. She climbed the stairs up to the porch and opened the door.

"Tal, HB," she said warmly.

I shook my head. "Don't bother. I heard your fight."

Her face dropped. She reached out to touch my shoulder, but I shrugged her off. "I don't like this," I said. "I feel like I'm being blamed for something that I had no say in. Like you guys are pretending to fight about me when you're really fighting about you."

Mom tried to reach out for me again and I dodged her. "Don't," I said.

"Taliah. Come on. It's complicated."

I pulled open the door to the porch. "You keep saying that, but you never explain anything." I walked away as she called out behind me. In my mad dash to get away from Mom, I ended up bumping into Julian.

"Tal," he said.

"Forget it," I said before he could say anything else. "I heard everything. Including that you wanted nothing to do with me when you first found out. When I was *five*," I spat.

"Look," he said, and shoved his hands into the pockets of his jeans. He shifted his weight from his right foot to his left. "It's not like you think."

"Let me guess, it's complicated?"

"Exactly."

I shook my head. "I'm tired of hearing that." I looked up at him again and felt hot tears building in the corners of my eyes. I walked away.

"Taliah! Please!" he shouted after me.

I waved my hand over my shoulder to let him know I needed some space. I walked quickly away from the farmhouse. So quickly that I was almost jogging, which made me winded, which made me not notice Toby until he called out to me.

"Hey there," he said. "I know you're dying to see me, but there's no need to run."

I laughed a little as I caught my breath. I put my hands on my sides. "Sorry. It was just a lot back there." I gestured toward the farmhouse.

He nodded solemnly. "I imagine."

His sincere look of understanding made me feel like an ass. "I'm actually not talking about Tom."

Toby raised his eyebrows. "Oh?"

"Yeah. My mom's here."

"Oh," Toby repeated, but this time as a declaration instead of a question.

"Yeah. And she and Julian have been . . . I don't know." I was about to say more, but I stopped myself. "But never mind. I don't know why I'm going on and on about it."

"Hey," he said, and put a reassuring hand on my shoulder. "You aren't going on and on."

When I didn't say anything else, he said, "Hey, you want to get out of here for a little?"

I did. I so did.

"I do," I admitted. "But am I awful if I leave right now? You know, with everything that's going on?"

He gave me a mischievous smile. "I bet they could do without you for a few hours."

"You really think so?"

He nodded. "Yeah. I do."

"Okay then."

"Okay then," he repeated, and motioned for me to follow him.

II.

"Bertha?" I asked.

He laughed. "Can you imagine any other name for her?" He was referring to his bright red pickup truck.

"I don't know," I said. "I guess I'm not very well versed in the naming of pickup trucks."

"Oh. Well, it's an art."

"I'll have to trust you on that."

"Please do," he said, glancing over at me. His eyes were warm, and the farther away we got from the Oliver farmhouse, the better I started to feel.

"You're always outside," I said.

He looked amused. "Is that a question?"

"Yeah," I said. "And an observation."

He pressed down on the brake as we came to a red light. "I don't really know how to answer that."

"Why? I mean, what do you like about being outside?"

"Everything," he said.

"No. Seriously."

The light turned green and Bertha lurched forward. Her engine let out a low rumble. "I don't know."

"Come on. Yes, you do."

"You're right. I do. But you're going to make fun of me."

"No, I won't. Give me a chance."

"Simplest answer is: I like trees."

I fought back a laugh. "That's your answer? Trees?"

"See? I knew you'd poke fun at me."

"It's not that there's anything wrong with trees, I just thought you'd have a deeper answer. Like something philosophical and transcendentalist."

"Naw," he said, his cheeks a little red. "Best way to explain it is I like trees."

"And what do you like so much about them?"

"They're good listeners. And they know how to let go." Toby parked Bertha in front of a building with a neon sign that read OAK FALLS CLASSIC LANES.

"Explain?"

He took the keys out of the ignition. "The way they lose their leaves in the fall but then regrow them in the spring. I think we could stand to learn a lot from trees. They're resilient. And they're always growing. You see, I lost my dad in October. I remember sitting by the window, watching the trees slowly lose their leaves. And then I remember a sad, long winter. But come spring, I watched as the trees sprang back to life, and it gave me hope. I learned a certain type of grace from the trees. The way they just let things go, knowing that there is always something new on the horizon. I know that sounds cheesy, but when I was six, it really had an impact on me."

I smiled at him. "I like that."

"Really? I figured you would have some smart reply to make about it."

I shrugged. "Nope. I like it. I really do. It sounds like I could stand to learn a lot from trees."

He gave me a smile. "I think you could."

"So," I said, focusing my attention on the neon sign. "Where are we?"

"The best bowling alley in Oak Falls."

"Bowling?" I let out a dramatic sigh. "Really? I'm not athletic at all."

He got out of the car and quickly slid around to my side to

open the door. He held his hand out to help me with the high step. "You don't have to be athletic to enjoy bowling. You just have to be a good sport and enjoy greasy pizza."

I took his hand and a slight jolt went through me. I stepped down from the truck. "I can get into greasy pizza."

We walked inside and Toby got us set up with shoes and helped me select a ball.

"The trick," he said, "is to pick one that's heavy enough that it will do the job, but not too heavy that you won't be able to get a good spin on it."

"So bowling is another thing you love? How does it rank compared to trees?"

"Below," he said, smiling. "But not that far below."

We had our lane to ourselves. He typed my name in as "TAL" and put himself in as "TOBY."

"Hey," I said. "Why do I get an abbreviation and you get your full name?"

"Because I wasn't sure I knew how to spell Taliah correctly."

"Am I the first Taliah you've ever met?"

He nodded. "I hope you won't hold that against me, though."

"Not as much as I hold your no-swearing rule against you."

He laughed. He picked up his ball and bowled it down the

lane. He knocked down an impressive number of pins. Toby was clearly no stranger to the bowling alley. He grabbed his ball off the ball return and bowled his second turn. A spare. He did a goofy dance in celebration.

"Stop," I said. "You're gloating before you even see how bad I am."

"I don't know," he said. "Carter and Brady are some mean bowlers. And you have those Oliver genes. I wouldn't count you out yet."

I didn't actually perform as badly as I thought I would. Toby still squarely beat me, but I managed to not make a complete fool of myself. After we'd bowled one game, Toby went to the concession stand to get us the greasy pizza that he had promised. He returned with two large cheese slices on paper plates.

He handed one of the plates to me. I took an appreciative bite, chewing through the melted cheese.

"See?" he said. "Told you the pizza was good."

"You said it was greasy. You never said anything about good."

"Greasy is basically synonymous with good."

"I don't know if that can be universally applied," I said, and took another large bite. "Probably just with pizza."

"With pizza for sure," Toby confirmed. He took a bite of his pizza and then asked, "So your parents are fighting?"

I set my half-eaten slice back down on the paper plate. I blotted my hands with a napkin. "It feels weird to refer to them as my parents."

"Okay," he said. "Let me rephrase. Julian and your mom are fighting?"

"I don't know if 'fighting' is the right word. My mom is doing everything in her power not to talk to him."

"That's rough," Toby said.

"Yeah. And I overheard some . . . stuff today."

"Stuff?"

"I think my mom might have told Julian about me when I was five."

Toby's eyes widened a little and he took a deep breath. "*Pamplemousse.*"

"Yeah. What the hell, right?"

"Are you sure that's true?"

I shrugged. "I'm not sure of anything right now except for the fact that all they seem to want to do is fight. Or do whatever weird passive-aggressive non-fighting thing my mom seems into. And I just feel like they're using me as an excuse for all of their bickering. When really what they're truly upset about has little or nothing to do with me. And for some reason that makes me even more pissed at them. Which I know sounds crazy self-involved—"

"No. I get it," Toby assured me.

"Really?"

"Yeah. Really. I mean, whatever problem they have clearly resulted in a big problem for you—your dad being kept from you."

"Yeah. I don't know," I said, and stared down at my bowling shoes. "But sorry. I don't mean to bore you with all of my family drama."

"You aren't boring me," Toby said gently. "You can talk to me."

Typical me would've shut up. Eaten her pizza. And gotten through the rest of the night by being amiable, but definitely not open. But I surprised myself. I wanted to keep talking to him. And that felt good. It felt really good.

"Okay, fine," I said.

"Okay, fine?" His face looked hopeful.

"You want to know what else has been bothering me?"

He put his hands on his knees. "Yeah. Lay it on me."

"My grandma"—and then I quickly corrected myself—"Debra. Yesterday she told me this theory she has about how all of us have multiple versions of ourselves. So like we aren't just one static personality. We all have different sides."

Toby nodded.

"And that the tricky thing about love is learning to accept and cherish all the versions of the person you love."

"Makes a lot of sense to me," Toby said.

"But the thing that bothered me is I don't think I do have multiple versions of myself. I'm just Taliah. And just

Taliah isn't even that interesting. She's just . . . well . . . sort of ordinary. And I want to be a musician. I don't think I've told you that because I didn't want you to think I was some lame girl imitating her dad."

"I wouldn't think that," Toby said softly.

"But you know what I mean. Anyway, I'm worried that the reason Julian has been able to craft so many incredible songs is because he has all these versions of himself. Like the Julian his mom describes is really different from the Julian I've seen. Even the glimpse I got of how Julian talks to my mom seems different from the Julian I've come to know. And I'm starting to really worry that I'm just not an interesting enough person to make art, to write songs that will matter to other people. I don't know how you go about cultivating these different selves. I feel like I've hardly found my one self, how am I supposed to go about collecting multiples?"

Toby's lips twitched. I could tell he was fighting back a smile. I stared back at my bowling shoes. "You think I'm silly, right?"

"Yes," he said. "But not in the way you think."

He leaned in toward me and reached for my hand. He held it, gently pressing his palm against mine. "Taliah. There are very few people I've met who I've found more interesting than you. Lost and found, remember?"

I nodded, a fluttery feeling building in my stomach. "You know, these are the kind of moments that I used to roll my eyes at when I read them in books."

Toby smiled knowingly. "Really?"

"Yeah," I admitted. "But it feels different when it's actually happening to you."

He leaned in even closer, not letting go of my hand.

"Those scenes," I continued, "they just seemed so . . . unrealistic. Like how can you instantly know with a person? But here I am. Talking to you in a way I don't really talk to anyone."

His fingers interlaced with mine. "I think with some people you can just tell you're going to have a history with them. Even if that history hasn't happened yet."

The fluttery feeling in my stomach grew. But something about what he said made me think of my mom and Julian. I wondered if it had been like that for them when they first met—that somehow they just knew that they were going to matter to each other.

"What?" Toby said.

"Nothing," I said, my voice barely above a whisper.

"No. I can tell something else is bothering you."

"It's just . . . it's upsetting that it seems like all of the songs Julian is famous for are so loved because of his sadness. Like doesn't it suck that it seems like he owes his whole career to

271

the fact that my mom broke his heart into smithereens?"

Toby's forehead wrinkled with thought. "You know what?"

"What?"

"I don't think what people are responding to in those songs is the sadness, Taliah. I think it's the love."

III.

Julian was waiting for me right when Toby dropped me off.

"I'm sorry," he said. He was standing near the entryway to the back porch.

"For what?"

"Well, for everything. But in particular for being scared when I first found out about you."

I looked at him and he seemed more vulnerable than he ever had before. Even in the hospital, I hadn't seen him seem this open. This raw. All of his rock star persona was gone. He was just a guy. My dad.

"I didn't know how I was supposed to feel," he continued. "I'd never gotten over your mother, you know? But I had taught myself how to live with it. I'd developed coping mechanisms. And then, learning about you, it opened up all those old wounds. I got scared. I ruined my chance. And I'm so sorry for that."

I paused for a long time. "You found out when I was five?"

He tipped his head back and sighed. "Yes. But . . . I was an idiot."

I stared at him.

"And when you got my letter?"

"I was an idiot again."

"That's starting to become a common refrain," I said.

"I know. And I'm sorry. I'm so sorry, Taliah. I'm tired of being an idiot and a coward. I don't want to hurt you anymore. I'm going to try to be better, you know?"

I looked down at my sneakers. I was silent for a long time. I thought of his famous pause in "That Night."

"Tal?" he said.

"I know," I finally said, quietly.

"Do you?" His eyes searched mine.

"Yes," I said. "I do."

"Plus," he said, a small smile snaking across his lips, "I had no idea how great you would be. I was such a clueless idiot."

I laughed, suddenly feeling very self-conscious.

"No, I'm serious," he said. "You're so great."

He reached out to hug me, and I let him. I didn't know if I quite forgave him yet, but I understood. And somehow understanding felt even more important than forgiveness. "Thanks, Dad."

I felt his whole body tense. He squeezed me tighter.

DAY FIVE

*(In Which I Learn How All Endings
Are Also Beginnings)*

I.

I woke up to my mom sitting on my bed.

"Geez," I said, startling and propping myself up. "Creepy much?"

Mom smiled at me. She reached out and grabbed my hands. "I'm sorry. I didn't mean to scare you."

I yawned. "How long have you been sitting there?"

"A while," she admitted. "I've been thinking—"

I wrinkled my nose. "About how it's complicated?"

She nodded. "And about how I need to explain my choices to you." She let go of my hands for a moment and sighed. "The thing is, I wish I had some dramatic story to tell you."

I blinked. "What?"

"You know. Something that would make my choices obvious to you. Explain everything." She shook her head and stood up from the bed. She began to pace across the room. "But it isn't like that. Over sixteen years ago, I made a choice. And it was a choice driven by grief and shame and fear. A whole lot of fear." She briefly met my eyes. "And I'm not proud of that. And I think, well . . ." She paused.

"Mom?" I urged.

"I think one of the reasons it's taken me so long to talk with you about this is because I was ashamed of how much of my decision was driven by fear. And I didn't want you to grow up believing that was the best way to make decisions."

I thought about how she had taught me to be so guarded and cautious. How she'd raised me to be suspicious of new people. "But you did," I said quietly. I didn't want to hurt her feelings, but I was tired of tiptoeing around the truth. I was so tired of it.

"I know," she said, letting out another heavy sigh. She sat back down on the bed. "I was torn because I also didn't want you to make the same mistakes I did. I never wanted you to trust the wrong people."

"Do you think you were wrong to trust Julian?"

Mom gave me a small smile. "I don't know." Her face went blank like she was remembering something. "After all these years, I'm still not sure."

n the days following the news of her mother's death, Lena spent most of the time feeling like she couldn't breathe. There was a physical ache in her throat. It was as if her lungs felt guilty for still working when she knew her mother would never inhale or exhale again.

"Let me go home with you," Julian pleaded with her every night.

But she'd shake her head. She couldn't go to the funeral. Not in the state she was in. She couldn't face her family. Lying to them about her career and her studies over the phone was one thing; lying to their faces was completely different.

"You're going to regret it if you don't go," Julian said to her as he held her, whispering into her hair.

"You don't get to tell me how I'm going to feel," she snapped, and pulled away from him.

But he was right. She did regret it. And she tried to nurse her regret by attending more of S.I.T.A.'s after-parties and social functions.

But the parties only made her feel worse. They amplified her feelings that an insurmountable gulf was growing between Julian and her. She, the grieving nobody whose artistic pursuits were going nowhere, and he, the rock star who was growing more popular and beloved by the day.

She hated that she resented his success. It made her dislike herself even more. She felt like she had disappointed her mother, and now, she felt as though she was disappointing Julian. She felt stuck in a cycle she couldn't escape: her jealousy made her upset, and the more upset she got, the more jealous she became.

It didn't help that at these parties she saw how many girls flirted with Julian. And how he flirted back. She was convinced he had cheated on her. Or if he hadn't, that he was on the verge of it, which somehow seemed even worse, in the way that the anticipation of something awful is sometimes worse than the thing itself.

Whenever she'd raise her concerns to Julian, he would shrug her off. He'd get annoyed, offended. Downright self-righteous.

"Lena, I've tried to do everything for you. And it's never enough," he would say, and then would leave the room in a huff.

And that was the problem. Nothing was ever enough. And she wasn't sure why.

At the last party she attended, she got there after Julian. She looked around for him and found him near the tiki bar, surrounded by girls. One of them, in a pink cocktail dress, was practically pawing at him.

She felt possessive. And then she hated herself for it. She made her way to the bar and ordered a drink. The bartender handed her something very tropical. Very Miami. She hardly ever drank, but she gulped it down in three sips.

"Whoa, there," a guy she didn't recognize said to her. "You're Julian's girl, right?"

She nodded tersely.

"I'm one of the new sound guys. Joel." He stuck out his hand. She shook it reluctantly.

"Your boy's a big star. He's got lots of new friends," Joel said. She could smell the alcohol on his breath.

She watched Julian put his arm around the girl in the pink cocktail dress. She was only a few feet from him, but he didn't see her. That was the problem. She felt like he never saw her anymore. She felt invisible.

And she was tired of it.

She hadn't crossed the Atlantic Ocean to feel invisible.

She thought about what her mother would think if she could see Lena now. And she knew her mother would be deeply disappointed, ashamed even.

That's when Lena knew what she was going to do. She would leave.

She would reclaim her life. She would become a doctor like she had promised her mother all those years ago when she'd boarded the plane to America. Maybe not the type of doctor her mother had expected, but it would be something.

And something was better nothing.

II.

When Mom finished talking, she looked emotional. She wasn't crying, but somehow that seemed worse. Like she was still holding all of it in. I thought about the sadness that oozed out of Julian's songs and realized that it wasn't only his sadness to own. It belonged to Mom too.

"So you left?"

"Yeah, HB, I left," she said, her leg brushing against mine. I scooted over to give her more space and she wrapped her arm around my shoulder. "At the time, it seemed like the only thing to do. I didn't like the person I was becoming."

I wondered if Debra had been partially right. That a

big part of love is learning to accept different versions of the person you love, but that it's also important to love the version of yourself that the person you love brings out. That sometimes it's possible to love someone fully, but still need to leave.

That seemed heartbreaking to me. And that's how I knew it was true.

"It was the most difficult choice I've ever made," Mom said. "Well, second most difficult."

"Leaving Jordan was the most difficult?" I asked.

She shook her head. "I didn't know about you when I initially left. But then a few weeks later I . . . well, I discovered I was pregnant." She leaned into me, resting her head against my shoulder.

"Did you think about telling Julian?"

"Of course," Mom said quickly. "There were many times that I was so close to calling him." She took a sharp breath. "And when you were five, I did."

"Why then?"

She moved her head away from my shoulder so she could look me straight in the eye. "I'm not sure, really. I think you had just done something—made some expression or something—that was so quintessentially Julian. And something cracked open inside of me. I guess it made me miss him."

"So you called him?"

She nodded. "And after a few moments of talking to him, I knew it was a mistake. We fell into our old pattern of accusations and arguments. I could sense the fear and uncertainty in his voice, and I didn't want to bring that fear to you. You didn't deserve that.

"You see, Taliah," she continued, "I made the initial decision I did not because I thought Julian would be an awful father, but because I didn't want to raise you in an environment with constant bickering. I didn't want you to see me as a person who was always jealous and disappointed." Her eyes met mine again. "It was a selfish choice. I know that. But at the time, it felt like the best one. I really thought, and honestly I still do think, that I was a better mom because I was able to do it on my own terms."

I straightened my spine so I could sit up more in the bed. "And as I got older, you never thought about telling me the truth?"

She reached for my hands again. "Oh, Taliah. Of course I did. But the more time passed, the guiltier I felt. And I didn't want you to see me as a liar, and I thought the best way to prevent that was to keep you from knowing the full truth. I was so scared of losing you." She gripped my hands like she was afraid I was about to disappear right in front of her.

"I'm not asking for you to forgive me right away, but I'm asking you to try and understand why I did what I did," she pleaded.

I returned her grip, squeezing her hands in mine. "I understand," I said slowly. "It makes me sad, but I understand."

She nodded a little and reached out to stroke the back of my head. "You know, I've been so worried about this moment for years. I knew that someday you'd discover the truth. And I knew it was closer than ever when you started to ask questions about Julian Oliver a few years ago. But now that this moment is here, now that everything is out in the open, I actually feel better."

I gave her a small smile. "Yeah," I said. "We should probably work on that, huh?"

"On what?"

"On opening up more."

She nodded again and a few tears finally spilled out of the corners of her eyes. "Yeah. We probably should."

III.

Mom kept her promise and let us stay for the memorial. Aunt Sarah's house was in a more developed area of Oak Falls. Unlike Tom and Debra's, her house didn't sit on a plot of rolling acres. It was a squat white brick home on the end of a cul-de-sac.

She'd organized the backyard for the event. Serving dishes of various dips and casseroles were laid out on a table on the deck, and her husband, Todd, was manning the grill, flipping burgers and hot dogs. She'd set up a small microphone near the edge of the deck and explained that later, she thought people could get up and share their favorite memories of Tom.

There was already a good crowd of people in the backyard when we arrived. I didn't recognize most of them, but I did spot my cousins nursing root beers and chatting under a shady oak tree. When they saw me, the twins gave me a halfhearted wave and it felt like progress.

"It's nothing fancy, but it's something," Sarah said to us when she arrived. "I thought we all needed something."

"It's wonderful, Sar," Julian said.

"It's lovely," Mom agreed.

"I know I told you yesterday, but I'm so glad you're here, Lena," Sarah said, and I could tell she really meant it.

Mom gave her a gentle smile and rubbed the small of my back.

I saw Toby standing in the corner by himself. "I'm going to go say hi to a friend, okay?" I said to her, and walked in his direction.

"How are you holding up?" Toby asked me as I approached.

I shrugged. "Overwhelmed. But somehow kind of content. I feel like for the first time in a long time, I'm exactly where I'm supposed to be."

A look of satisfaction passed over his face.

"I don't mean—" I said quickly.

"I know, I know. But I can't help but agree with that proclamation."

"Really?"

"Really," he said. "And you know what else?"

My stomach flipped a little. "What?"

His dark eyes twinkled. "If this wasn't the memorial for your grandfather, I would kiss you right now."

My cheeks burned in the best sort of way as he reached for my hand. "And I should've kissed you last night at the bowling alley. And the night before in the woods. But again, the timing," he continued. "But I've decided to forget the timing." He wrapped his arm around my waist and pulled me close to him. He leaned down and kissed me gently on the lips.

My whole body thrummed. The kiss was quick, but somehow it felt infinite.

As Toby pulled away, the backyard got dramatically quiet. I worried for a moment that everyone was staring at us, but as I looked around, I saw that the crowd was focused on Julian, who had made his way up to the small microphone. He tapped his fingers against the mic.

"So you'd think by now I'd be used to speaking in front of a crowd of people," Julian joked. The crowd let out a slight laugh. "But right now, I'm unbelievably nervous." His eyes found mine and he smiled. "But I'm going to try to fight through my nerves because I want to tell you about my dad."

The crowd leaned forward in anticipation. And somehow, even though I knew what we were all there to commemorate was an ending, it also felt like a beginning.

As Julian paused, his mouth hovering above the microphone, I briefly wondered if the reason so many people loved his songs was because he invited the listener into a place of certain uncertainty, a place that allowed for sadness and anger. And love.

A place that felt a whole lot like both an ending and a beginning.

And I felt like I'd finally reached a place similar to that myself. A place with lots of unknowns, but that was somehow okay. Better than okay, even.

I was ready for my beginning.

ACKNOWLEDGMENTS

Endless thanks as always to my wonderful and wise agent, Brenda Bowen. I'm beyond lucky to have you in my corner. Much gratitude to the rest of the amazing team at Greenburger Associates, in particular Stefanie Diaz and Wendi Gu.

So much gratitude to my very patient and very smart editor, Alessandra Balzer. Thank you for shepherding this story through its many iterations. I feel so lucky to get to work with you and the rest of the incredible team at Balzer + Bray/HarperCollins. Thanks also to Kelsey Murphy for her sharp eye and all of her help. Additionally, thanks to Jenna

Stempel for designing another jacket that I absolutely love.

Many thanks to all of my friends who held my hand and offered guidance during the drafting process of this book. In particular: Emery Lord, Kate Hattemer, Kim Liggett, Becky Albertalli, David Arnold, Adam Silvera, Kristan Hoffman, Alexandra Perrotti, and Erica Kaufman. Thank you to Kayla Whaley for reading an early draft and providing invaluable feedback.

I'm forever grateful to everyone who helped take care of Lillian so that I could meet my deadlines—Kirsten Hahn, Linda Warga, and Kathleen Warga. And of course my mother, Patricia Nazek, who indulged all of my ramblings about possible plot points.

Much love to all of my family. I'm very fortunate to be the recipient of so much support. Gregory, Lillian, and Juniper: I love you more than words can say. You're my little big world.